FINDING S.A.M.

FINDING S.A.M.

BY MARY BLECKWEHL

WITH ILLUSTRATIONS BY BERAT PEKMEZCI

ONE ELM
BOOKS

Egremont, Massachusetts

One Elm Books is an imprint of Red Chair Press LLC
www.oneelmbooks.com

Discussion Guide available online.

Publisher's Cataloging-In-Publication Data
Names: Bleckwehl, Mary Evanson, author. | Pekmezci, Berat, 1986- illustrator.
Title: Finding S.A.M. / by Mary Bleckwehl ; with illustrations by Berat Pekmezci.
Other Titles: Finding SAM

Description: Egremont, Massachusetts : One Elm Books, an imprint of Red Chair Press, LLC,
[2021] | Interest age level: 009-013. | Includes discussion questions. | Summary: "Zach has plenty on
his mind as middle school starts, without worrying about his older autistic brother who lives in his
Superman shirt and counts the neighbors' windows. In an effort to cope, Zach imagines he has a
'super-cool' brother who offers advice that turns tragedy into acceptance"--Provided by publisher.

Identifiers: ISBN 9781947159488 (library hardcover) | ISBN 9781947159495 (softcover) | ISBN
9781947159501 (ebook)

Subjects: LCSH: Brothers--Juvenile fiction. | Autistic children--Family relationships--Juvenile
fiction. | Imagination--Juvenile fiction. | CYAC: Brothers--Fiction. | Autistic children--Family
relationships--Fiction. | Imagination--Fiction.

Classification: LCC PZ7.B61677 Fi 2021 (print) | LCC PZ7.B61677 (ebook) | DDC [Fic]--dc23

LC record available at https://lccn.gov/2020931247

This book is a work of fiction. Any references to historical events, real people or real places are used
fictitiously. Other names, characters, places, and events are products of the author's imagination,
and any resemblance to actual events, places, or persons, living or dead is entirely coincidental.

Main body text set in Minion Pro 13/19.5

Printed in Canada

1020 1P FRNSP21

MIX
Paper from
responsible sources
FSC
www.fsc.org   FSC® C016245

For Bill, our children, and our journey

When you're 12, are you too old to have an imaginary brother?
—Zach

"What do you think about starting middle school tomorrow, Zach?"

Dad asks me no more than one deep question a year, and I think this is it.

"I think someone in this town should figure out how to stuff the ninth graders into the high school so Braden can be in a different school than me."

My parents yank their necks 180 degrees and give me a look like I've just announced I robbed a bank.

Hey, you asked!

That night Mom makes us all go to bed early. "Mom, I'm in seventh grade now. I don't have to be in bed by 9:00." I look at Dad for backup, but he has his nose in the paper.

"It will be easier to get your sisters and brother down

if you all go to bed at once."

Dad!

I lie in my bed staring out my window, thinking about what it will be like to have Braden in my school. It shouldn't matter that I have a brother who happens to have autism, but it does.

Finally my body relaxes. I feel heavy. Swaddled. Until some idiot shoves me. Now there are more. Six or seven of them poking and taunting. I back away. "Your brother's a retard! Your brother's a retard!" they chant. A gang of boys who, oddly, look like me is shoving me closer and closer to the edge of... something. I hear rushing water somewhere below. "I can't swim!" More people come to push me. Mom, Dad, Bart...

I jolt awake, certain I'm in a free fall. My arms and legs are thrashing around in my blankets, and my heart feels like it's leaping out of my chest.

Once my body settles down, I sense someone else in my room.

Oh, not again.

He's back.

2

I can't let Zach go to school without a haircut.
What's gotten into that kid?
—Mrs. Berger

Hazard Middle School is exactly 1.1 miles from our house. If you lived more than a mile away, you could ride the bus. But who wants to ride the bus when you're in middle school? My BFF Phinney pointed this out when I complained about having to walk that far.

My problem with walking isn't really the distance. It's that my autistic brother will be with us. For the past two years Braden rode the little bus for kids who wouldn't do well on the regular bus of bullies and flying food. But since we'll be in the same school this year, Mom got one of her bright ideas to have us walk together. And that means seventh grade at Hazard Middle School could be painful.

"Hey, no problem!" Phinney told me when I mentioned Braden would be walking with us. "Braden's my bud!

3

Don't sweat it, Zach." I love the Phin-man's positive thinking, and I hope he's right. Maybe walking with Braden won't be a big deal.

But this morning, I'm not so sure. Braden is one thing. But Sam, my imaginary brother, is back. Shaky legs carry me to the shower.

I feel tired and on edge. Middle school will be different than elementary school. Mounds of homework every night. Sports. *Girls*! And on top of all that, I have to walk my ninth-grade brother to school? How embarrassing. My friends are definitely going to think that's weird.

I stare into the mirror. Where does my part look better? I try it on the right. Then the left. I add water to my comb and push it all straight back. I can't start out by looking like a goon on my first day. My mousy brown hair is bleached from the summer sun, and the waves aren't as wavy anymore. At the last minute, I change from a brown polo shirt to a faded blue tee. Sam gives me the thumbs up.

Stop it! Sam's not real.

"That shirt looks great, Zach. It matches your eyes."

I didn't know Mom was in my room. And there is Braden right beside her. Oh great. An audience.

I feel my face grow warm. "It's just a t-shirt, Mom. Guys in middle school wear t-shirts."

She tousles my hair and laughs. "Better grab some breakfast. Phinney will be here soon."

Braden follows her out like a shadow. He's wearing one of his Superman shirts and carrying his sticker collection in a plastic tub. "D-d-d-oes my shirt match my eyes too, Mom?"

"Absolutely, Dear. You look great!"

As I put on my shoes, I get an idea. Braden is solidly into routines. Maybe distancing myself from him from day one would make for a good routine. So I break it to Mom as I walk into the kitchen.

"Mom, I'm going to be leaving early for school every day so I can get some extra homework time in during homeroom. Braden can just keep riding the bus like he did last year."

"Why, Zach!" She is smiling so wide I can see her black dental fillings in the back of her mouth. "I love the way you are already thinking about your grades!"

Yes! She's finally agreeing with me on something.

I smile back just as wide. In fact my cheek muscles probably don't know what they are doing.

"Well, I don't want the teachers to think I'm a slacker or something."

"That is wonderful!" She gives me a mom hug. I pull away before she gets all mushy. I mean I'm going into seventh grade.

"However, you can get up early and do homework here." She glances into the hallway where Braden is struggling with which shoe is left and which is right. "We want to give Braden some independence, and one of his goals this year is to walk to and from school."

I pick up on the word independence. "Great!" I sound like a pig squealing over his feed. "Then he can be independent and walk alone to school."

Mom giggles. "And how do you think that will go?"

She's right. I can just see Braden getting to Emerson Street and counting the cars all day and never getting any further.

I want to be honest with my mother and say, *"Braden embarrasses me and my friends make fun of him. How do you think I'm ever gonna go to college and get a girlfriend if she sees that Braden is part of the package, and I have to stay home to cut his toenails instead of going on dates?"*

Instead I say, "Geez, Mom! I'm just a kid, not Braden's

parent. That's what I feel like sometimes, you know. Like I'm his third parent *and* his babysitter!" I realize too late that I'm yelling.

Mom turns wide-eyed and her lips quiver.

Immediately I wish I could take it back. I mumble, "I guess it'll be fine," and try not to sound like my whole middle school career is sliding into the sewer.

Mom hugs me again and turns toward the sink. I bet my baseball career that she's crying. She's a tough lady, but her son yelled at her and... her other son has autism. And then there's Sam. If she only knew.

Ugh! Mom's upset, I'm ticked, and Dad's nowhere around as usual. Braden's the only one good here. And probably my twin sisters, who are already in their happy second-grade place at Hazard Elementary.

"Hey Berger Brothers! Are we ready for the big time?" Phinney calls through the screen door.

"Let's go, Zachary!" Braden has finally figured his shoes out and is all perky. "Wait until I show Miss Cynthia my new sticker collection." He's been waiting to show her that collection since June, for Pete's sake. Maybe I'm being selfish, but I do wish he could go to a different school. I know it's the law to have special needs kids get all the support they need in regular schools, but have lawmakers thought about brothers like me? Apparently there's no law about what *we* need.

The three of us head toward Emerson Street. I stick the granola bar that Mom handed me in my backpack. She has no clue that the middle school doesn't give a snack break.

"Won't it be great to have different teachers every hour?" Phinney is pumped.

"I know. That rocks!"

"Teachers don't rock," Braden says in his flat-as-a-squashed-bug voice.

"Sure they do, man!" Phinney slaps Braden's arm playfully. "In elementary school, teachers want to know every detail about you so they can help you with your self-esteem. But teachers in middle school don't have time for hand-holding. They just need you to score well on tests so they look good, which means they ROCK!"

This is good news.

I laugh at Phinney's comment but inside I have a sad, sick feeling as I watch Braden walk a few feet in front of us. His arms and hands are flapping and he's deep in conversation with himself. I glance up and down the street. Thank goodness none of my baseball friends see me with Braden. One block before we arrive, I feel Sam feeding me an idea.

Sam is supposed to stay in my bedroom!

I try to shake him off but I can't.

"Hey Braden," I say. "Mom says you're supposed to try things on your own. Every day when we get to this street, you can walk on ahead." Braden loves the idea and takes off smiling like he's going to the national sticker conference. He even stops flapping.

The butterflies are working hard as I watch him go. Braden's been going to this school already for two years and knows it better than I do. No big deal.

As we near the school, I can't believe the hordes of kids piling off buses and moving toward the school entrance like cattle. When I look toward Braden, I don't see him. Instant panic and then relief move through me as I see him waving at his old bus driver.

"Hi Carl!" he yells—and then bolts in front of a moving bus the size of Texas.

I notice everything at once and it's all big and loud. I bet Superman feels this way.
—Braden

"BRADEN!! LOOK OUT!"

The entire middle school universe hears my scream. But Braden doesn't move.

"NO!" *Braden's gonna get run over by a bus and die on the first day of school.* I suddenly want to die, too. My mother will kill me anyway, once she hears I left him alone.

Panic grips my throat. The dark angry water is swirling beneath me, and I'm losing my grip on the cliff. I'm back in the same old nightmare, only this time I'm not asleep.

Luckily the bus driver has been practicing stopping on a dime and misses Braden.

Someone hauls me back onto the cliff where I lie, trembling. "Thank you, Sam," I whisper.

Phinney gives me a confused look. "What did you just say?"

I shake my head. "Nothing. I'm just… nothing."

I keep walking toward the school but feel a weight on my back like I'm carrying the whole autism nation. No matter how I try to distance myself from Braden, I can't. I was praying middle school was going to be different. He's my brother, my *real* brother, but—geez!

And Sam? I thought he was long gone. I can't let him back into my head.

The first person I see when I enter the school is Peter Salzmann, my crazy neighbor. *Could my day get any worse?*

"Your brother okay?" He must have witnessed the near miss.

"Fine." I mumble my family mantra and head straight to the bathroom to decompress. Standing in one of the stalls, I lean my forehead against the coolness of the door. Breathe. Braden nearly got run over by a bus. I let that sink in. Breathe. This is the same kid who makes my mother back into every parking spot, the one who never flushes the toilet even when he goes number two and is obsessed with light bulbs. How many more episodes of insanity will I be granted before the autism police come and carry him away? Or me.

Despite nearly getting my brother killed, the rest of the day goes fine. Mostly.

When I get to my homeroom, I can't believe my luck. Miss Thompson is no longer an elementary social worker. She is my homeroom teacher *and* my life science teacher, which means she's the first person I'll see in the morning and the last person I'll see before I go home. *SCORE!*

I purposely don't look at Miss Thompson when she starts telling us about our schedule. I just want to hear her calm voice explaining the ins and outs of seventh grade. I grew to love that voice when I had my one-on-one time with her in elementary school. I seldom looked at her then either. I just listened to that silky voice. And now, even though she is talking about homework and high expectations and detention, her voice makes me feel like someone is feeding me chocolate intravenously. I'll want to get to school on time every day just to hear that voice.

Phinney notices me dreamily staring at my desktop. He whispers, "Tell your mom that coming to school early for homework is mandatory."

I smile and relax further into my seat.

• • •

First hour is art class with The Pin. His real name is Mr. Flynn. Some call him Flynn the Pin or just The Pin because of his bald, little head.

Phinney is in my art class, as well as a new cute girl. *Wait! That's mousy Monica Monahan. Wow! What happened to her over the summer?* In sixth grade she was just a regular girl with a pointy, little nose, and now she's—not mousy at all. In fact, she reminds me of those girls on *America's Next Top Model*. Well, the one time I watched it.

Next, there's English with Nicotine Nancy (aka Mrs. Harris). She is saying something about how we'll be reading *To Kill a Mockingbird* this year. As she strolls by my desk, I get a waft of cigarette smoke and practically gag. Maybe there's a sequel called *To Kill a Student* starring Mrs. Harris.

Monica is in this class too. She is seated across and one desk ahead. Perfect observation point! Phinney gives me a thumbs up. Now this is the way middle school should start!

Monica turns and catches me staring. I feel my face

burning and look away, but not before I see her smug smile. She moves her legs closer to the aisle and crosses them—all the easier for me to see them. How am I going to get a decent grade in here with this distraction? I wonder if she'd like to go to the movies with me sometime. Like I'd ever get the nerve to ask her.

Third period I have study hall, which is a joke the first day of school since there's no homework yet. Mad Marlys, the old hippie, is in charge. Her real name is Mrs. Moser, and she has three black hairs on her chin that wiggle when she talks. The word is she won't retire, which is okay because she provides a lot of entertainment for middle schoolers.

I have heard stories of students being very cruel to Mad Marlys and taking advantage of the fact that she's old and just plain wacky. Last year, a student declared Mad Marlys Day and got kids fired up to wear wigs and clothes that resembled hers. They drew black hairs on their chins with markers and pretended they couldn't hear. Kids can't resist feeding on people like her, even if they come from decent homes where the parents make them go to church and write thank-you notes after birthday parties.

Cockroach texts a bunch of kids in study hall and tells

them to turn the volume on their cell phones on high and call someone in the room at exactly 10:40. Cockroach got his nickname because he is very small for his age, and you could see how someone might easily step on him. His real name is Carl Van Holt, and he is trouble with a capital T, as Dad would say.

At 10:40 over twenty phones start ringing. Having no phone I can't participate in the cruel and unusual fun. The ringtones are as varied as the kids who own them: James' mother yelling, "GET UP, JAMES!" A motorcycle revving. Some heavy metal song.

Mad Marlys is not only crazy, but half deaf. She has one hearing aid but apparently could use another, as it takes her a while to notice the "ringing." And when you're older than dinosaur bones, I suppose your experience with electronic devices is minimal. She asks a couple kids near her if they have a transistor radio on. James asks, "What's a transistor radio?" which sets off some snickering.

Then Harley Stinson's phone rings and everyone jumps. His ring tone sounds like a foghorn, and Mad Marlys definitely hears it.

"Everyone out!" she yells breathlessly.

What?

She thinks it is the fire alarm and starts muttering, "I can't believe we're having a fire drill on the first day of school. Nobody tells me anything."

She instructs us to quickly proceed out the side door of the school and meet by the flagpole. We do what we are told, laugh at Mad Marlys' expense and wonder how this will play out. Practical jokes don't always end well in schools. Detention is usually the prize. Maybe with Miss Thompson.

It takes Mad Marlys a few minutes to realize there is no one else outside except our class. The goody-goody, Judith Wattington, tells Mad Marlys that someone was just playing a joke on her, but MM doesn't hear or chooses not to. She looks confused until Judith goes right up to her and repeats her explanation on high volume.

"False alarm!" she yells in a deranged kind of way.

When we get to the door we exited from, it is locked, so we traipse to the main entrance. The principal gives us an odd look as we parade by his office. Cockroach gives him his best angelic wave, and we all return to study hall.

When the bell rings we empty into the hall, laughing so hard I'm worried we'll all have internal injuries. Something tells me I'm not going to get a lot done in study hall this year. I also anticipate a lot of fire drills.

• • •

Math is next. No Monica. But the class is loaded with guys from my baseball team, including Bart "the Bully" Hurtle. He's still *numero uno* on the popularity charts and still a jerk in my book for how he treated Braden last summer at our first baseball game. Thinking back, I still regret not pummeling Bart. If Sam had been a real brother, he would have taken ol' Bart out. But Sam wasn't real, no matter how much I wanted him to be.

Braden had been sitting in his usual spot on the ground by the dugout that day, thumbing through his notebooks and bag of stickers. That's when Bart got off the bench and wandered over. "Hey, big Berger brother. You know you're wearing your shirt inside out? Do you do that so it matches your brain?"

I may not like what Braden does, but no one talks to my brother that way.

Bart then turned to me and asked, "Berger, what's up with your brother anyway?"

Sounding a lot more confident than I felt, I said, "My brother has autism, Bart. What's your brother's excuse?"

The rest of the guys liked that one, but Bart didn't. He

somehow poured a bottle of ipecac into Braden's soda, and I ended up missing two innings to help Dad get Braden into the port-a-potty. Bart had to have planned that, as you don't just carry vomit-inducing stuff in your bat bag.

The awful part was the way I felt that day at the ball field. I was ashamed that I was thinking the same as my friends did. I wished Braden would just stay home.

When we got home I laid it out for Dad. "We've got to do something about Braden. He's ruining our lives. Don't you see the way people look and whisper when they see us coming? We'll always be known as *that* family with the autistic boy!"

Dad simply said, "Other kids misbehave on purpose. Braden does it because he doesn't understand social cues. Besides, no one cares what Braden does."

I did! I didn't want my brother to be the laughing stock of Hazard Middle School. I wanted a brother like Sam, not Braden!

When you're almost thirteen, you care about a lot of things—and one of them is who you hang out with. I wanted to tell Dad that. I had plenty to tell him, like how I wanted to invite my friends over, and that Braden embarrassed me when he did goofy stuff like flapping or counting windows. But Dad got a call from Hazard Technical College, where he was Security Director, and had to run off to see why one of the college dorms had smoke rolling out of it.

I would really like to fit in for a change.
—Zach

After tripping down memory lane, I am jolted back to the present by Mr. Piper, my math teacher. It's a night-and-day difference between him and Mad Marlys. He runs his class with military precision, so there's no horsing around. Cockroach is in here but he wouldn't dare act up with Piper in charge.

While Mr. Piper chats with the principal near the door, we take advantage and talk to each other, except for the girl in front of me who must be new. She stares straight ahead. I can't see her face, but her hair is this really deep chocolate color and so soft-looking that I actually reach out and touch it.

Maggie Martin is the chocolate-haired girl's table partner and is blabbing to Bella Storlie across the aisle. "I'm trying out for cheerleading, and I'm going to join the science club and maybe speech team which means I need to change my violin lesson. I don't know when I can get homework done because I don't have any study halls. Do you?" It's enough to hurt my ears.

I'm at a table with Justin Christianson, a pitcher on my baseball team. Calvin Jespers and Bart are across the aisle.

"What field is football practice going to be on?" asks Justin. I notice his voice has started to change.

"Field two," Bart replies. "Hey Zach, wanna sit with the guys and me at lunch?"

I nearly choke on my own saliva. "Sure!" I'm a little too enthusiastic. I wonder what this is about. Bart's basically ignored me and treated my brother like dirt since I was in third grade, and now he wants to eat lunch with me? I should have answered, "When pigs fly." But this is middle school, the land of cliques and popularity. I would really like to fit in for a change, and following Bart might be my ticket.

Mr. Piper wastes no time with rules and goes right into a lecture on the importance of math in our world.

"We'll have assigned seats starting tomorrow." Naturally. No seventh-grade teacher in his right mind would let us pick our own seats, not even the "Mad" one.

By lunch I'm famished. I don't see Phinney anywhere. I forgot to ask when he ate lunch. It's probably just as well, as Phinney doesn't think much of Bart and his posse. Of course, they think Phinney is a nerd, which is true. But he's an awesome nerd. Other than Phinney, I haven't had any friends to my house for a while. They make fun of Braden and it's hard to stomach. Especially Bart Hurdle, the self-proclaimed king of the in-crowd. A few still invite me over, but I don't feel like hearing them remind me I have a strange brother. I already know that.

• • •

While we're standing in the cafeteria line inhaling the smell of spaghetti, Bart makes sure everyone hears him. "In social studies, I asked Ole' Pick n' Flick when it was going to be snack time, and he told me 'grade school is over young man.' When I told him I was feeling faint-like, he suggested I get up earlier and eat breakfast. No sympathy for the starving newbies here at Hazard Middle School."

"You mean he didn't flick you one of those fleas he pulls out of his beard?" laughs Calvin.

This gets a chuckle from all of us, and I'm feeling good. I move my tray along to the dessert counter where homemade cookies and chocolate pudding catch my eye. I think of Mom's attempt at baking and how her cookies are always flat and mostly burnt. There are at least half a dozen signs stating ONLY ONE DESSERT PLEASE!

Cockroach grabs two, but one of the kitchen ladies snatches his wrist. "Don't be one of those greedy seventh graders!" she advises. I guess the Dessert Police are in full force here at HMS.

We head toward a table. Supermodel Monica and her girl group are at a nearby one giggling and looking five years older than the boys. It must be the makeup.

I'm the last to reach the table and realize there's not a chair for me.

"Zach. There's an extra place with us." The supermodel has come to my rescue! She directs Amalia to move down and pulls the chair out for me. What's with the red carpet treatment for Zach? First, a Bart invitation and now one from Monica. Is it my t-shirt or has my luck changed?

Bart shrugs. "Go for it."

I take Monica's offer and start shoveling my spaghetti in. Thankfully I am sitting beside Monica and not across from her so I don't have to be distracted by her blue eyes. The girls chat on as though I'm not there, which is a relief.

I have little experience talking to girls other than my sisters, especially when I'm wrangling slippery pasta.

I'm ready to dive into my chocolate pudding when I hear a familiar voice. "Zachary, I want to sit by you."

Braden has pulled a chair from somewhere, and before I can even reply through my spaghetti-packed mouth, he jams it between Monica and me. In a nanosecond he loses his grip on his tray, and I witness what could be the end of the shortest seventh-grade career in the history of HMS.

So much for luck.

5

**I feel like I'm standing on the edge of
a rocky cliff, and I'm losing my footing.
—Zach**

Braden's tray tips in slow motion onto Monica's head. She gasps and bolts up from her seat as the spaghetti sauce hits. Her shriek explodes across the cafeteria. *"Ahhhhh!* What are you doing?! *Ahhhhh…!"* She flaps better than Braden.

Red sauce drips down her face as she sputters and wipes the guck from her eyes.

I feel myself coming unglued. It's only the first day, and it was starting to go so well. There is throbbing inside my ears, and the roaring returns like a wind tunnel through my brain. I see Sam's face. He looks disappointed in me. I shake the vision off.

I jump up, grab my napkin, and start wiping Monica down, but she backs away gasping. She is steaming. There's a huge blob of chocolate pudding on her once-white shorts, and I wonder if the Our Lady of Perpetual Light School across town takes late registrations. Or would they just take Braden? Permanently?

Monica's girl gang is screaming, and the guys are howling with Bart pointing at Braden. Every eye in the cafeteria is on us. Suddenly, there's silence. I stumble back and steady myself against a trashcan. An avalanche-sized pain in my head strikes near my temples. First the near hit by the bus, and now Braden coats the next supermodel with spaghetti sauce. I am losing my footing on the rocky cliff once again.

Braden isn't at all fazed. I should go and help him clean up.

Monica shrieks me back to attention. "Look what you've done to my clothes!" She's directing her ear-splitting comments at Braden.

It's not his fault, Monica. Please don't yell at him. He can't help it. Autism. I'm sorry. SAM!

I step forward. "I'm *so* sorry, Monica. It was an accident." It's all I can offer.

Monica spins and glares at me. I swear I see flames rolling from her nostrils, which are flared wide. I back up even further, taking the trashcan with me. She looks like a bull ready to charge. The raging animal shakes her head, and the spaghetti flies. More shrieking. This time, it's from her friends who are getting sprayed. Man, you can't make this stuff up.

A girl is squatting down to clean up the mess. Excellent, a Girl Scout among us. Braden stands watching her, oblivious to the snickering. Girl Scout picks up Braden's fork and napkin and uses them to scoop the spaghetti from the floor onto his tray. She directs Braden back to the cafeteria line for a new tray of food. Good, someone's taken control.

When Girl Scout returns with a rag to wipe up the remaining mess, I recognize her. It's the girl with the incredible hair from math class!

Miss Supermodel spins and marches out the door with her new spaghetti-and-pudding ensemble, followed by two members of her entourage. And I'm not hungry anymore. I see Braden has a new tray and is sitting with a teacher assistant. Girl Scout has disappeared.

I concentrate on gaining control of my lungs. This is like drinking from a fire hose. Too much, too fast.

As I walk to social studies, I see Monica leaving the building with an adult who looks an awful lot like her.

Her mother, I am guessing. They are actually giggling. Girls are weird. Shrieking and spewing fire one minute, laughing the next.

• • •

Mr. Dunphey teaches social studies. "Let's spend this hour getting to know our table of contents," he says.

This guy could come in a close second behind Braden in a monotone contest. He strokes his long thin beard, adjusts his wire rim glasses. And is that a wig on his head or a dead opossum?

Mr. Dunphey picks something out of his beard and rubs it against his black corduroy pants. Whatever it is, he isn't getting it off his fingers, so he flicks it, and it lands squarely in the wastebasket. Now I can see what Bart was talking about and where Mr. Dunphey gets his nickname: Pick n' Flick.

Phinney looks at me from across the aisle and gives me his "Did you just see that?" look. He holds up two fingers and I choke back laughter. Before the class is over, I count five more two-pointers. Social Studies just got less boring with a basketball sideshow.

Next up is Phys. Ed. with Mr. Presell. We sit on the bleachers and listen to his rules. "If you chew gum, you write yourself an invitation to see the principal." I can see his chest moving in and out with each breath. He is badly overweight. I hope he doesn't have a heart attack. He takes a huge drink from his water bottle, sucks in a breath, and moves on to the next rule.

Now I see why he's called Puddles. His shirt isn't just damp under the armpits. It's soaked from his pits to his belt. I feel short of breath just listening to him huff and puff his way through this.

I allow my gaze to roam the tops of the heads in the rows in front of me. Bart, Maggie, Amy, Jordan, Phinney, and the Girl Scout. I feel like I should thank her, but I don't really want to think about that lunch disaster.

Twenty minutes into Puddles' rules, the gym door opens. I stiffen when I see who walks in. Braden and another student walk to the bleachers with a teacher assistant and sit down. Really? Braden's in one of my classes? I hear the rushing of water below my feet and clamp my fingers around the edge of the bleachers. A headache around my right eye has started. It never dawned on me that Braden could be in any of my classes. I don't remember anything else Puddles says other than, "If you apply these rules, you get an A."

The grand finale of the day is in front of me. I will not let Braden ruin it for me. I walk into life science, and there she is, Miss Thompson, wearing a green blouse that matches her eyes and a bright smile. She covers her class expectations, and I feel my muscles relax with each word. Her face is flushed and damp with perspiration. She's probably had a long first day of warding off all the boys eye-dogging her.

It is warm in the science room. Of course there's no air conditioning in this wing. Maybe Dad would like to tackle that issue. He is always ranting about the school board and how cheap they are.

Miss Thompson smiles right at me. "There will be a lot of homework in this class, and if anyone is having trouble with it, I recommend you stay after school for tutoring."

I anticipate needing a lot of tutoring.

I don't know what people want.
They keep changing.
That's why I like my stickers.
They never change.
—Braden

Mom tries to talk me into walking Braden home every day before football practice. This is so ridiculous! "Mom, I'm going to need a lot of help in science, so I will probably stay for after-school tutoring."

"Zach, you surprise me. You want to stay after school for tutoring?"

You don't remember having hormones, Mom? Evidently the science teachers weren't hot when Mom was in school.

"All right. I'll pick Braden up after school." Victory count: Mom, 100. Zach, 1.

Braden and I set off for our second day of school.

"Braden, you have to walk with me all the way to the front door today."

But Mr. Independent isn't having it. He flaps and whines, so I finally tell him I'll buy him some new stickers if he stays on the sidewalk and doesn't run in front of the buses. Now I have to figure out where to buy superhero stickers.

"You're figuring it out, Berger!" Phinney gives me a fist bump, but Sam is rolling his eyes.

I sit safely with Bart and company at lunch. "I see they have your brother back in his cage, Berger." Bart motions to Braden sitting with his T.A. Other kids who look like they might be tray spillers are sitting with Braden. I want to get away from Bart, but where do I go? The guys I want to hang out with are sitting with him. And the girls aren't likely to invite me back to their table.

Monica is back with a new outfit. Amalia informed me that Monica hit the mall following yesterday's spaghetti storm.

"Hi, Zach! You think today's cafeteria entrée will match my new clothes?" Monica twirls to show me every side of her perfect self before she sits down to eat.

I have to hand it to her for being a good sport. I think she might even like me, and I've given a solid five minutes of thought to asking her if she wants to play tennis sometime. But Bart Hurtle announces he's asked her to a movie. Makes sense: most popular boy dates most popular girl.

For all the talk on the first day of school about reading *Mockingbird*, I figure Mrs. Harris would be handing it out today. But she says we need to work up to that kind of content, and assigns *The Outsiders* by S.E. Hinton.

The Outsiders is another old book, published sometime in the 60s. Smart aleck Rudy Daley asks Nicotine Nancy a worthwhile question. "Why do we have to read stuff that's older than our parents?"

Nicotine Nancy leans over and breathes into Rudy's face. "Because it's classic literature, Ralphy." Rudy's face reddens. He's either mad that she called him Ralphy or ready to keel over from her tobacco breath.

Our first assignment is to do an author study. When I Google S.E. Hinton, I find out the S stands for Susan. Ugh. This is no doubt going to be a girl book, assigned by a girl teacher. And why do authors do that? Use their initials instead of their name? J.K. Rowling, E.B. White. Like they're trying to hide something. Maybe when I turn in my next paper I'll sign it Z.J. Berger. But somehow it sounds more like a rapper than an author.

I read that the author was fifteen when she started writing *The Outsiders* and eighteen when she got published. My interest barometer goes up a few notches.

I forget sometimes that I like reading. There's so much other fun stuff to do, like sports and video games. But once I start reading an awesome story, nothing else exists, not even Braden. Writing is the same way. It lets me go places away from everyone, including Braden.

Mrs. Harris introduces the characters and assigns a chapter a night starting the second week of school. With characters named Ponyboy and Sodapop in the story, I'm skeptical about how awesome it will be. But this is school, and you read what you're told, not what you like.

**Other people like hugs and malls
and people. Not me. I feel smothered.
–Braden**

On Monday night I start reading the first chapter of *The Outsiders* before bed. Suddenly I hear, "Zachary! I've called you three times. Did you set your alarm last night?"

"Huh?" I roll over and see the sunlight streaming in under my shade. The clock says 7:22 a.m., but my body is telling me it's still the middle of the night. I sit up slowly.

"Your hair looks funny," giggles Eva from the perch she's taken in my chair. I squint at her.

Sisters! I point at my door. Eva sighs and leaves.

I see my *Outsiders* book on the floor and lean down to pick it up. It's open to the ninth chapter. I don't know what time I fell asleep. All I know is that I wanted to keep reading.

Ten minutes later, Mom tosses me a muffin and

shoos me out the door. "Get your hair cut after school today, Zach."

All day I think about that book. Are there kids like that? Without parents? Living by themselves, poor and ending up in street gangs? I look around my English class. What if I knew a kid who had to fight just to survive, someone from the wrong side of the track, fighting people like me, who have parents and food and normal stuff? Well, normal except for Braden.

I think about the poem in chapter five, the one Ponyboy says to Johnny.

Nature's first green is gold,
Her hardest hue to hold.
Her early leaf's a flower;
But only so an hour.

Then leaf subsides to leaf.
So Eden sank to grief,
So dawn goes down to day.
Nothing gold can stay.

Nothing gold can stay. It's like a haunted spirit whispering to me.

WHOMP! I jolt awake. Nicotine Nancy has dropped a dictionary on my desk. "Mr. Berger. You may sleep in my class, but snoring is where I draw the line." The whole class gets a gratifying laugh. "Remember your assignment tonight is to read chapter two. We'll discuss it tomorrow."

I just want normal.
–Zach

It is finally LINK day! I can't tell you how long I have waited for this day. LINK day is what our little town is known for—when every seventh grader in Hazard, Indiana, gets assigned a ninth-grade student buddy called a LINK. Since Braden is lousy at sports and Dad is always too busy to do guy stuff, I need someone normal to hang with. This is the day I'll be matched with that great normal someone.

The ninth graders—also known as freshmen—walk into our social studies classroom led by their teacher, Mr. Sawyer. It's crummy to say, but when I see Braden, I am bummed. I was hoping his homeroom would be matched up with a different class. His eyes are all excited when he spots me, and I can't help but notice how much he looks like me. Same athletic frame, blue eyes, wavy blond hair. He has one of his dozen superhero shirts on and immediately comes over to my desk and whispers, "Are these energy-saving light bulbs?" I shrug and motion him away.

I sadly wonder who would get him for a LINK. He'd drive them crazy with questions. He'd ask about their light bulbs and phone numbers. He asks Mom and Dad ten times a day about the lights in our house and reads the phone book like it's a bestselling novel.

One by one the ninth graders announce who their seventh-grade LINK is. And as each is announced, it becomes obvious that my dream LINK isn't going to happen. Only two ninth graders remain to make their LINK announcement—Braden and *that* girl. Pimply, plump, and obviously arrogant. I feel bad for Emily Larson who would be stuck with her. Getting my own brother as my LINK buddy would be a gift in comparison to what Emily would be in for.

It is Braden's turn to make his announcement. I look up and force a smile. He fumbles with his piece of paper, opens it finally, and squeezes his eyes shut. *Just say my name, Braden.* Sometimes he has trouble getting his words out. He is staring at the ceiling. I bet my new bat that he is counting the ceiling tiles.

Braden looks confused and is picking at his Superman shirt. He steals a rare look at me. Eye contact isn't his thing. I nod at him. Sometimes he needs that—a visual cue to let him know everything is fine.

It isn't fine for me, but what choice do I have? The teachers choose the LINK matches, not students. On the bright side, maybe Braden and I will make history as the first LINK brother duo. We'll be famous and get into the Guinness Book. Well, probably not, but I need to find the positive in all this.

I glance at Phinney. He had gotten a perfect match in Carter Fields. Both are science wizards and funny in a nerdy kind of way.

"Braden, introduce yourself," Mr. Sawyer coaxes.

Still in his trance and staring at the ceiling again, his flat voice barks, "M-m-my name is Braden. My seventh-grade L-L-LINK is…"

Are those tears in his eyes? I've never seen him get anywhere near crying. Mom always says he doesn't really know how to show emotions.

Finally Braden whispers it. "M-m-m-my LINK is Emily."

"No!" My response ejects me from my chair.

Braden's words ignite my thoughts like a spark on dry grass. Sometimes he gets things wrong. It's the autism talking. But he knows me—his own brother! Why would he say Emily? She's a girl. Boys are never linked with girls.

"Braden, it's me," I pleaded. "*I'm* your LINK." I never thought I'd see the day when I was begging to be his *anything*, let alone his LINK. But the alternative isn't possible.

"No, Braden's right," Mr. Sawyer says. "His seventh-grade LINK is Emily."

Which means my LINK is…

OMG!

Some people are afraid of the dark. I'm afraid of lights.
—Braden

I feel something shake loose inside me. Through a sea of confusion and snickers, the remaining ninth grader in the front of the room looks right at me through her thick glasses. Her snobbish, nasal-sounding announcement makes me want to peel her words right off me. "I am Annabelle Doreen Jackson and *my* LINK is you, Zachary Berger."

"Unbelievable," my voice squeaks. *That* girl is my LINK? How can I make sports history with her? "I get stuck with the odd duck."

Embarrassment isn't a big enough word to describe the situation. I slide down fast and far in my chair, causing my head to smack hard on the back of it.

I hear girls screaming and shake off my brain fog just in time to get a look at Braden. *No no no! Braden!* My

42

brother has Mr. Dunphey's meter stick. His "just-for-teacher" meter stick.

"I want Zachary as my LINK!" Braden shouts as he mounts the desk and begins to bash a piñata tied to the ceiling panels. I see the horror on Mr. Dunphey's face. We had just papier-mâchéd the piñatas for a Spanish culture project. Someone grabs the stick from Braden, but it's too late. As candy rains down, I squeeze my eyes shut. This is not the way I pictured this day.

My temples pulse and things grow deathly quiet. Everyone stands still as statues, including Braden, who has dismounted the desk. Mr. Sawyer moves toward Braden and corners him between the wall and a desk.

"Don't do that!" I shout.

Braden's face is the picture of panic. His eyes are desperately searching for a way to escape. Back and forth, up and down. When he looks up a second time, the lights grab him. His eyes are glued to one flickering fluorescent light.

Braden grabs a chair and mounts the desk again. He beats the flickering light to oblivion until the two teachers manage to pull him down, where he collapses into a seizure.

I open and close my hands a lot.
It helps me focus on what I'm doing.
—Braden

The principal, Mr. Aspen, and the nurse show up. Once Braden comes around, they walk us to the nurse's office. "I'll call your mother," she says.

At least I'm not being sent back to class and to Annabelle. Maybe Braden and I will be famous for ruining LINK day.

The only light on in the nurse's office is a lamp. For some, this might have a calming effect. But I see Braden zeroing in on it, and it's all I could do to breathe normally. I close my eyes. When I open them, Braden is pulling at his eyebrows and occasionally stopping to flap his hands. Once when Eva asked Mom why he does that, she said, "It's Braden's way of processing things. It helps him put the pieces back together when he's falling apart."

Well, things are certainly falling apart today. There

won't be anything left of those eyebrows, and after the stunt he has just pulled, Braden may as well flap himself to Uzbekistan.

The principal greets my mother like she has just arrived at a party. "Thanks for coming Mrs. Berger."

He turns to me and Braden. "Why don't we start by hearing what happened."

Braden has shut down like a dead cell phone, so it's up to me.

Sam's whisper hisses through my skin. "Give it to 'em, Zach. Tell them. Tell them!"

"Braden stole something from me today." The words spill out of my mouth.

Everyone stares at me like I've just spoken in Japanese.

"I d-d-did not steal."

I start my defense. "We were told the purpose of LINK is to give us a good middle-school role model. We all wrote essays explaining our interests and our teacher promised a good match. I got that nasally, pimple-faced…" I draw in a deep breath. "I got Annabelle Doreen Jackson! Who in here thinks that's a good match?"

I am shouting, and Braden is burying his face in Mom's lap, so I tone it down.

My voice speed goes from 60 to 100. "Everyone in this town talks this program up. Parents, teachers, kids—they tell us the stories of how some of the LINKS become life-long friends. The Indianapolis TV guys even were here last year. Today was the day I was going to be matched with someone so awesome that Wikipedia would have to add a new entry for it!" My jaw is tight, and I barely recognize my accusing tone. I realize I'm standing. I take a breath and sit back down.

"Braden and I had no idea our classes were being matched up. Do you think someone could have clued us in on that?" The principal is leaning in, looking like he's ready to pounce.

I have a whole lot more to say, like the fact that Braden and whoever made the matches had ruined this day for me. That I'm so tired of having to make excuses to my friends as to why my brother acts the way he does, even though I know he can't help it. That I just want a normal brother for ten seconds to see what it feels like.

Something is in my eyes, making it hard to see. The same thing is in my throat.

I hiss the rest to keep my voice from breaking into pieces. "Don't you people here know anything about autistic kids? That they need to have a little advance warning about things or life can take a dangerous turn?"

I am about to remind them about the time we were 30,000 feet in the air on our way to Colorado when Braden's video display didn't work on the plane. He insisted on opening the plane's door so he could walk to Best Buy and get it fixed. It has nothing to do with today's catastrophe, but my mind keeps whirling back through all the Braden crises.

I look at Mom and fight the flood. "And Mom, did you know Braden goes postal when he stares at lights?"

Her red, wet face shakes back and forth. "No, I didn't."

I never even knew Braden was different
until I was eight. The mailman told me.
—Zach

On the way out of HMS, I see Phinney sitting on the steps. He has been my best friend since second grade when he ate his science experiment in front of the whole class. Swallowing a goldfish was the gutsiest thing I'd ever seen, and I couldn't stop laughing. That's the best thing about Phinney. He makes me laugh, and heaven knows I need to laugh.

But today I am not in the mood for one of Phinney's jokes or his famous "Don't sweat it" lectures. I move as fast as I can to the backseat of our rusty van, where I squeeze between our two Irish setters, Hank and Beulah. They wag their tails and are thrilled to see me. I lean against Hank and feel some of the nutty stuff drain out.

Braden hits his head on the car roof, as usual, getting in the front seat.

"I'm too b-b-big in this car." His voice is monotone. "We should get a Jaguar. I like Jaguars. Zachary, do you like Jaguars?"

I ignore him.

"Zachary."

He asks me three more times if I like Jaguars. "Yes."

A Jaguar would be nice. Our junkyard beater is nearly as old as Braden and just as embarrassing.

My twin sisters, the redheaded duo, are in the middle row which is stained with who knows what.

"What took you so long?" impatient Carly demands. She and Eva had been waiting in the school office.

Wars take a long time, Carly.

On the ride home, I stare at the back of Braden's head and think back to second grade when Mr. Fahey, our mailman, told me, "Sorry, you've got a brother who isn't right." It took me a couple years to see what he meant. The stuff Braden does and says means nothing is ever normal in our house, and after today, it won't be normal at school either. I close my eyes and picture Mom driving us far away to a place where no one cares if I have a brother who makes my life suck. A place where it's fine to have an imaginary brother.

49

When we arrive home, Mom flies into her multitasking mode. She reaches for all the empty gum wrappers in the car console, picks up her purse, puts her water bottle in it, settles her sunglasses back in its case, notices one bow of her glasses is loose, sets the glasses down, pulls out a notepad, and scratches a note, presumably about getting the glasses fixed. Then she rips the note off and holds it between her teeth.

I watch all this from the backseat, wondering if my sisters are going to move sometime in this century so I can get out.

"Zach, please bring in the mail, and when you come back through the garage, honey, will you sweep it out? The dogs must have got into the garbage. It's a mess," Mom tells me. "But first, you can put your backpack in the house, and hang it up on the high peg, not the short one or Beulah will get into it again."

Anything else?

"And don't sweep out the garage in your new jeans. Run up and change before you do anything. And you might as well make your bed while you're up there, because for some reason you forgot this morning."

I didn't forget.

"And don't forget to feed Hank and Beulah."

Dad had brought us the two red-haired puppies on the day my sisters turned one. Or maybe two. I guess he thought Braden and I needed a present, too. Dad is a good egg, even though he's not around much.

Our dogs used to be named Rex and Roland until Dad read me the *Hank the Cowdog* books. We laughed ourselves silly over Hank's life and his love for a beautiful collie named Beulah. After reading those books, I insisted we change our dogs' names.

Mom turns and looks at me still seated in the backseat. "Zach, are you all right?"

"I'm fine." I don't sound fine.

"Fine."

I will punch a hole through this van roof if I hear that word one more time today.

She watches me for a few seconds. "Well then, what are you waiting for?"

For a genie to appear and for Braden to be miraculously cured.

I drag myself out of the car.

"Mom, can Eva and I go to the park?" asks Carly, twisting her red curls around her finger.

"Sure," Mom replies with a giggle. "Have fun girls. I'll have dinner ready in an hour."

Just like that, they skip off without one single chore. How I want to be seven again.

Mom reaches for her briefcase and lunch bag and begins stepping out of the car, but not before wiping down the dashboard. "All dusty again," she mutters.

Mom turns to Braden, who is rocking back-and-forth in the front seat. "Braden dear, please pick up the DVDs in the family room and put them back in their cases."

Braden flaps his hands. He doesn't like her idea.

"And no watching *Happy Feet* until the DVDs are back in their cases."

More flapping.

Mom only gives Braden one thing to do at a time. He didn't inherit Mom's multitasking gene. No male has that gene.

Mom goes in the house and starts dialing the wall phone to call Grandma. Yes, we still have one of those. Actually, three: one on every floor, including the basement. We apparently are holding out to get in the Guinness Book as the last family on the planet to own wall phones. I made the mistake once of asking, "Could we PLEASE get a cordless phone?"

Dad said he liked the wall version and went on to enlighten me with the history of the telephone when he was a kid. "The party line was the first version of Facebook. If my parents wanted to learn the latest gossip they just picked up the phone and listened in on the neighbors' conversations."

Groovy, Dad.

While dialing, Mom rummages through the mail and sees a bill from the dentist office. She spits out the note about fixing her glasses and hangs up the wall phone. I smile, imagining Grandma's face as she's left wondering who just hung up on her.

"Zach, when was your last teeth cleaning?"

"October," I lie. I know it's been over a year, but I hate that fluoride junk. So does Braden. He threw up after having that once. Ever since then, taking him to the dentist requires military intervention. And, if you have time, I'll tell you which army is needed when he has his annual blood draw.

Mom dials the dentist, continues sorting through the mail, and lets the dogs out through the patio door.

I pick up her cell phone. In theory, I share it with my

mother. That was the explanation when she told me I was too young to have my own.

"Mom, I know second graders with their own cell phones."

"I'm not their mother."

I use it to call Phinney. I want to ask if I can move in with his family until I find a permanent arrangement—say in Morocco—but he doesn't answer.

There are 102 windows in the houses on our cul-de-sac.
—Braden

Dad arrives home three hours early from work. He wears an expression that screams, *Heavens no, your mother didn't call me and tell me that my boys' actions in school today means that we should get out of Dodge before sunup.*

"Hey Zach!" Dad gives me a high five. He hasn't done that in months. Next he ruffles Braden's hair. "Hey Braden, where is Mom?"

"I am putting my DVDs away."

Braden never detours. One task at a time. He has to finish what he starts. A very respectable quality unless you're ready to head to the 7:00 movie, and Braden needs to finish putting his DVDs in order. And when I say order, I'm not talking alphabetical or by color or anything obvious. I mean Braden order. So we're used to missing the previews. And the first fifteen minutes of the movie.

When he is done with the DVDs, Braden heads to his room. "Skipping *Happy Feet* today?" I ask. No response.

After I finish my Cinderella duties, I go into Braden's room. I don't want to admit it but I take Sam along. I have been trying real hard to leave Sam behind, but he's like a magnet or a favorite blankie or something crazy I can't explain.

A certain amount of tolerance is required to walk into my brother's room. Braden has his favorite song playing: "Believer" by Imagine Dragons. The green army soldiers he and I used to play with are lined up around the room. They start on his desk, continue across the floor, and up onto the windowsill. They march under his bed and, where the little green guys come out from the other side, Braden has duct-taped a cardboard arch to the carpet. The soldiers parade under it and behind the door. A small superhero figure leads the entire brigade. And the family rule is: no one messes with Braden's army.

Braden doesn't look up. He seldom looks at anyone. Just one of the million goofball things about autism I guess. Braden was diagnosed with ASD when he was four. The letters stand for Autism Spectrum Disorder. The counselor at the sibling camp I went to with

Braden said, "Autism is a disorder affecting social skills, communication, and behavior."

I watch Braden write the number 172 on a page. He turns the page. 173. He's always counting something. The number of cracks in a parking lot, the number of times the church bells ring, even the number of age spots on Grandma's arms. The school psychologist says this is how he processes information.

Whatever. It's what he has to do, but there's no logic in it for me. It's just... odd. 174.

Braden has his sunglasses on. He always wears them in his room. He sits cross-legged on the floor and cradles a light bulb he's taken out of his lamp.

"What?" Braden notices I am there. The curls fall down his forehead and make him look younger than his fourteen years. 175.

"Nothin'. I just came to see how you are doing."

"Fine."

At the sound of his small, soft voice, I feel sad and guilty. I kneel beside him.

"Did you want to be my LINK, Braden?" I wondered if I should go there.

Silence. 176. Without looking up from his important

numbering work, he asks, "Who-who?"

He stutters when he isn't concentrating on his talking. Or when he is stressed or for no reason at all.

"Who-who would you pick Zachary?" he asks. He never calls me Zach.

My throat catches, and I have to concentrate on keeping my voice even. 177.

"Braden, if they lined up all the kids in the ninth grade on the fifty-yard line of the football field and I could only pick one to be my LINK buddy, do you know who I'd pick?"

"Me." There is no emotion in his answer. It is just there, like a shirt that's been ironed flat. 178.

I'm glad he doesn't look up at my wet eyes. He would want to know if I got hurt.

"Yea, you," I whisper. *A normal you.*

Downstairs I hear Mom and Dad talking, so I turn off "Believer," which makes Braden flap his arms. Dad has on his oldies station again. "Hey Jude" drifts up through the floor heating vent. Braden hums along, rocks back and forth, and makes up his own words to it. Hearing him makes me hurt inside. He is just doing his Braden thing. He is so full of *not-normal,* and it makes me angry that he has to be like this. Somewhere inside of him there is a normal kid—I just know it. I wish I could rip the autism part of him right out and blow it to bits.

We live in one of those old houses that has been "kept up nicely," as Mom would say. The floor heating vents have allowed me to eavesdrop on a lot of conversations.

"Hey Jude" ends and the radio gets turned off. Thank God. That old Beatles music is depressing. Mom and Dad are in a serious discussion about Braden's meltdown at school. It is as much a downer as the Beatles music.

"So you think the flickering light in the classroom caused Braden to have a seizure?"

"I'm not sure. But I think we should talk to Dr. Graham about it. Migraines and things like seizures can be triggered by flickering lights."

"Angie, Braden has autism, not epilepsy."

"Some people with autism can have seizures too." Mom's voice is a sad whisper.

I look at Braden to see if he is taking any of this in. He is still busy numbering his notebook pages. 205.

"Something happened when Braden stared at those lights today, Jason. Zach saw it and so did the teachers." The last words are barely audible as Mom chokes them out.

"It must have been awful." I hear a sickening sob from my mother.

I don't want to listen to any more heating vent news. I reach over and press repeat on Braden's CD player. "Believer" returns and Braden smiles. He sings along to it like it's the autism national anthem. 212.

In a stiff sadness I walk to my own room and leave Braden to his papers and numbers. I feel Sam close behind me.

Lying on my bed and staring at my Indianapolis Colts poster on the ceiling, I long to talk to Sam but fight it. Instead, I call Phinney. "Know any decent school I could transfer to?"

"The Lady of the Holy Pants and Perpetual Light School is across town." I knew I could depend on Phinney to make me laugh.

"Hmmm… that private school? That would set my parents back a bit to send me there. Would put a dent in the ol' college savings."

Phinney suggests a bit of advice. "Maybe returning to deal with a broken piñata won't be as difficult as the high expectations at Lady of the Holy Pants."

Mom calls us to dinner but I just pick at my food. Mom

is a lousy cook, and I'm used to that, but tonight it's worse than usual because it's seasoned with the disappointment of LINK day.

Carly whines about the spaghetti because it doesn't have meat in it. "What are these things?" She holds up a fork of chunks.

"Garbanzo beans," Mom tells her.

"Gross. Why can't we go to a fast food place to eat?" asks Carly.

"We didn't even have fast food when I grew up." Terrific—Dad and one of his war stories of life in the olden days.

"Why not?" asks Eva.

"Because *all* the food was slow."

Carly laughs so hard, spaghetti squirts out of her nose. Any other night this may have been funny to me. But I am still in a bit of a shock over the day's events and what tomorrow will look like when I return to school.

I wish I had a best friend like Zach Berger does.
—Bart

Girls have an odd perspective. After LINK Day, all the girls in my class think I am a hero. Maybe they just feel sorry that I am stuck with Allergy Annabelle. Luckily, the only time I have to spend with her is when we have game time on Fridays.

The first Friday we meet, Annabelle asks, "What's wrong with your brother?" This seems inappropriate to me.

"He's fine."

Annabelle glares at me and blows her nose three times. "I'm not stupid you know." Her voice is as irritating as fingernails on a chalkboard.

After her class leaves, I spend ten minutes sterilizing my hands in the bathroom.

Braden actually loves being Emily's LINK, and she is so patient with him. If only Braden hadn't looked at the light, it would have saved that piñata. I wonder to this day where all the candy went. Probably in Mr. Dunphey's desk.

Phinney tries hard to help me get over the whole LINK thing with his jokes and just being the Phin-man. His real name is Phinneas, which means mouth of a snake in Hebrew (according to Phinney). He says it's ironic his parents named him that because snakes don't talk, and he can't stop talking. I told him maybe there is a hidden message behind that. One day when he was going on and on about his name and the whole snake's mouth thing, I told him, "It's more likely you were named after Phineas on the *Phineas and Ferb* cartoon."

"What? The dude with the triangle head?"

"Yeah. You know how he and Ferb are always inventing junk out of stuff in their basement? You're always building stuff out of recycled junk and mixing chemicals in your bathtub and blowing things up."

"I guess. But I don't have a pet platypus named Perry. Although I'd like to have a pet who is a secret agent like Perry is."

"You can have Polly."

Polly is our talking parrot. I taught her to say 'Mad

Cow Marlys.' It sounds more like *man caw mouse*, which is just as well so my parents don't catch on.

Phinney's a super guy: kind of nerdy, but funny and kind. He has straight, jet-black hair that sails behind him as he runs. And can he run! His lungs must be supersized. I consider myself a better-than-average athlete and can run fast, but no one catches the great Phinneas McGee.

The best part about Phinney is that he doesn't care what Braden does or doesn't do. Phinney's famous line is, "It takes all kinds of kinds." I wish I had his attitude.

One day, out of the blue, he asks, "what would you rather have your brother be like? Bart the Great or Braden the Great?"

I laugh to hear my best friend refer to Braden as 'the Great'.

"Neither. Those are not even choices." Braden is… well, Braden. And Bart already thinks he IS the greatest.

"Oh, so you're picky, huh?"

"I just want Braden the Normal, Phinney. Is that too much to ask?"

I glance over my shoulder to where Sam is sitting. Phinney turns his head in the direction where I'm looking and gives me a questioning look. I have to be more careful.

I don't know what Phinney would think knowing I have this imaginary brother. But how great it would be if he was *real*. Sam the Great!

Autism doesn't hide; it isn't quiet.
There's no disguising it, and it
multiplies every time you try.
—Zach

Things happen in schools. You know, when you don't hand in your essay or math assignment, and sirens go off because it alerts your teacher to send you to the homework-help police.

But certain things are only whispered about, like folklore. Things that, if they happen at all, should happen in the deep, dark woods where only fairies live and magic potions repair the damage—not in front of your seventh-grade friends.

But if your brother is Braden Berger, there are no far-off places. Because autism doesn't hide; it isn't quiet. There's no disguising it, and it multiplies every time you try. It strikes and ricochets, taking everything in its path with it, including me.

Maybe it was because Braden was upset he couldn't be my LINK, or maybe his eyeballs stuck on that bright something on the ceiling and triggered an electrical explosion in his brain. Either way, it left me worrying that Braden's problems were worsening.

*I wish I'd gotten a picture of Zach's face when
I shot that first bullseye. I'd totally frame it.
—Grace*

Puddles needs to enroll in a physical education program of his own. When you're round and old, you could pull a muscle getting a drink of water. So I can't say I blame Puddles for choosing activities that aren't so strenuous. Like archery.

I doubt I'll like archery, because I like team sports. The only archery I've done is on my Wii, but this is the real thing. I mean, who has a real bow and arrow to practice with?

Puddles tells us we need a shooting partner. Oh Dear God, please don't put me with Braden.

Puddles has us count off by twelves, which sounds kind of dumb but, whatever. It's school. We get our orders and do them.

There are thirty kids in our gym class. We get to the

third round of counting off by twelves and stop at six because we run out of people. I am a seven.

"All right people. Find the other students with the same number as you, and go stand by them and act like you like 'em." He sounds as enthusiastic about this as if he was telling us to watch plastic break down. But I think it's because he's out of breath from talking.

"Most of you will only have two at a target, but some targets will have three."

I was paying attention when everyone counted. The other seven was Grace Elliott, the Girl Scout. I feel this nervous butterfly thing going on in my gut. I look out of the corner of my eye in her direction and see her looking at me. She was paying attention to the count too.

"You better learn to love this person because they will be your partner for the next three weeks, and don't even think of asking me for a change. I don't care if they smell. You're stuck with 'em."

Everyone chuckles except Puddles.

Mr. Presell moves so now Grace is in my line of vision. She doesn't look friendly, and I bet she stinks at archery. I hope I don't have to help her hold her bow or something weird like that. If I have to pair up with a girl, why can't it be someone friendly like Maggie or Abby? But at least I'm not with Braden.

"Now, if your partner fails to follow my rules and fires an arrow into your behind, let me know ASAP, and I'll make a reservation for them in detention." We all laugh again, and Puddles gives us a fake smile. His face is red and wet from perspiration. He pauses a while to catch his breath and then tells us how to shoot and score.

"The most important part is my whistle commands, and you know I love to blow my whistle. Let me demonstrate."

"One blast, shoot."

"Two blasts, get bows."

"Three blasts, pick up arrows."

"One long blast, STOP SHOOTING!"

Puddles gives his lungs a break.

"We'll have a written test on whistle commands on Friday. I better see a perfect score from every one of you, or you're looking at 50 push-ups."

Ugh.

On the other hand, I'd enjoy seeing Grace doing that. But she doesn't look strong enough to last through ten push-ups, let alone fifty.

Puddles emphasizes his golden rule. "Remember, people. Once you are done shooting, DO NOT RETRIEVE YOUR ARROWS. Wait! W-A-I-T." He's panting now. "Never, and I repeat, never go and pick up your arrows until I give the all-clear blast of three whistles. Why do I care? I don't really but my kids need to eat and in order to feed them, I need a paycheck. If I get sued by your parents because you have an extra hole in your body, I won't have a job, and my kids will starve to death."

We get the picture. Go get some oxygen, Mr. Presell.

I sense Sam's intuition and glance at Braden. Yes Sam, you're right. Braden is gonna have trouble waiting for that whistle.

We spend a long time practicing Mr. Presell's "Eleven Steps to Archery Success." Our shooting stance and how to nock an arrow onto the string, draw it back to the side of our face, and anchor a finger at the corner of the mouth, plus a few more I've already forgotten.

Grace and I don't speak. I never did thank her for helping Braden the first day of school.

Man, you need to stop thinking about Braden!

Sam's reminder distracts me. I need to leave Sam at home.

I didn't know fingers could sweat but mine seem to. The bow is stiff and feels foreign in my arms. But everyone's in the same boat. I am too preoccupied with my own bow to notice whether Grace or Braden are getting this. Luckily, Braden has a T.A. for this class.

"People. It's now time to put what we've learned into action and do some shooting."

Puddles blasts his whistle two times, which means one person in each group can pick up a bow from the rack and walk to the shooting line.

I think I better be a gentleman and let Grace go first, but she motions me ahead.

Fine.

When I hear the one-blast whistle, I take an arrow out of my quiver and glance toward Grace. She is watching me. *Geez.*

I place the bow on my toes the way we were taught. I remember my open foot stance position, nock the arrow, and hook the bowstring into the groove. Step by step, I go through Mr. Presell's shooting procedures, taking my time. I center my grip and raise my bow arm and drawing arm to eye level. My arms shake. I feel Grace's eyes on me and glance in her direction causing me to momentarily lose my concentration.

Other kids have already let arrows sail. There are whoops and laughter for targets hit or missed. I aim for the bullseye and begin moving my shoulder and elbow back. Man it feels tight. I release my grip. The arrow flies and barely catches the top of the target before slipping loose to the ground.

Oh well.

Many of my shots don't even hit the target. I shoot my last two arrows. The first one drops to the ground by my shoe before I try again and manage to get it to sail toward the target. It nicks the outside edge—the bottom one this time. It hangs on to produce a score.

This is kind of embarrassing.

I hear Bart laugh, "Hey Berger, remind me not to rely on you for food when we're called up for the Hunger Games!"

My last arrow manages to hit the outside blue ring for five points.

Okay, so I'm not Robin Hood.

Grace is up, and I'm relieved to stand back and watch her make a fool of herself too. I smile and give her my good-luck-you'll-need-it shrug. No smile from her but at least she isn't moaning for help. I mean this isn't the Olympics.

I was going to look to see how Braden was doing, but when Grace pulls out her first arrow, I notice her fingernails. They aren't painted and long like a lot of the girls', certainly not like Monica Monahan's. Hers are always some shade of shocking pink and have little gemstone sparkly things glued to them. Grace's are chipped, and her fingers and right hand are scratched and dirty.

Grace quickly pulls her first arrow up and out of the quiver onto the bow.

That's when I see it—a nasty two-inch scar on her left wrist. The rest of her skin is flawless.

Not bothering to check her stance or take her time with each step as Mr. Presell insisted, Girl Scout eyes the target. I know she is going to blow this. In one motion she sets, draws, aims, and shoots. Right into the bullseye.

My eyes nearly leave my head. Mr. Presell's booming voice bellows, "BULLSEYE on target seven," which causes a momentary ceasefire while kids look to see who nailed the first one. Cheers erupt.

"Beginner's luck," I mutter. Grace gives me a dirty look.

She probably took this class already at her old school.

"Berger! Maybe you better take her with you to the Hunger Games for protection!"

My face burns. Bart is a jerk.

Grace picks up her next arrow. I stare at her face and the way she draws the string to the side of her smooth cheek. Smooth, flawless motion! BINGO! Another bullseye.

No way.

"Hey! You're awesome!" says Abby Johnson, girl jock destined to be a pro something someday. Name a sport. She excels in it.

By now everyone stops shooting, even though we haven't heard the long whistle command. All eyes are on Grace, and they follow her third arrow right into the center of the target.

Whistles and applause flow through my stunned brain.

"Never mind Berger. I'm taking her to the Hunger Games myself!"

It's Big Mouth again.

Grace puts her bow down with no expression at all, and I don't know why, but I want to find out more about this Grace Elliott, her archery skills, and that nasty scar on her wrist.

I feel like I should say something.

Puddles honks the whistle three times, giving us the okay to retrieve our arrows safely.

"Way to go."

She smiles shyly. "Thanks."

Alert the media. She speaks. And smiles!

16

It's been such a relief now that Zach's old
enough to watch Braden and the girls.
—Mrs. Berger

"Just make sure you stay in the same room with him
all the time so he doesn't escape." Dad gives me the last
instructions before heading out the door.

It's like I'm taking orders on how to keep a mountain
lion in his cage so the neighborhood isn't terrorized.

My parents have "Back to School Night" at my sisters'
school, so I have to hang out with Braden.

"You don't have to feed or entertain him, just keep
him safe for an hour or so."

For the most part, it's easy "babysitting" Braden as
long as he stays in the house. For a couple years there,
he would slip out, and we had to have the police on
speed dial.

Tonight he's watching the Hazard city council meeting
on cable, so I wander up to my room with Dad's laptop to

check out archery tips on the Internet.

• • •

"Zachary Jason Berger, come down here right now!" Mom's welcome-home greeting blasts up the stairs.

They're already home? I fly down the steps. I swear I feel Sam flying beside me.

Ohmygod!

"Holy buckets!" It's Carly.

We all stare at the same thing. Braden has his bike in the living room. Or shall I say, his bike parts. The greasy chain is on Mom's white sofa.

Mom's gonna shoot him. Correction: Me.

"What are you doing, Braden?" Dad's voice sounds almost amused.

"Fixing my bike."

"Mmm… I see that." Dad squats down beside him, watching Braden's greasy hands work at getting his kickstand undone from the bike frame.

Dear Eva sweetly says, "I can help you fix your bike, Braden." I smile inside. I love that girl.

Braden has the contents of Dad's tool box dumped onto the new carpet, which unfortunately is closer to light tan than dark brown and now has greasy tools, nails, and a bunch of random junk, like wire and fishing hooks, spread out all over it.

Beulah is chewing on a tape measure, and Hank is licking one of the bike tires.

Mom walks to the sofa and carefully picks up the black chain with two fingers. It leaves a perfect figure-eight grease mark. I hold my breath waiting for the explosion. "Did you know he was doing this?" Mom looks at me for a sensible answer.

Oh sure. I actually suggested he ruin your recently remodeled living room.

"Mom, it's fine." I figure it's worth a shot to try her famous "fine" quote.

One look tells me she doesn't think so, and she fumes off to the kitchen, returning with a bunch of cleaning products and brushes. I reach for them, but she yanks them back and starts spraying something strong onto her sofa. It drips black streaks down the side of the sofa onto the carpet.

I may as well kiss my allowance goodbye, until I'm 30 or so.

Dad and I help Braden move his bike parts and tools back to the garage. Since Dad isn't very handy with mechanical stuff, he loads the bike parts into his trunk. "I'll have the bike repair shop fix 'er up like new for you, Braden." He gives Braden a pat and chuckles.

He's not your responsibility. Sam's words aren't that comforting.

Through our sophisticated heating vent intercom system I hear Dad tell Mom her white sofa was a ridiculous purchase. "I thought the same thing about that old motorcycle that you bought that still doesn't run."

Is it weird that I think about Grace so much?
—Zach

I can't see her wrists from where I sit in math.

Ever since archery started, I find myself thinking about this Grace a lot, which is a good thing because it means it's less time worrying about Braden or my obsession over a normal brother. A person isn't just naturally an archery expert. So where would a seventh-grade girl learn to shoot like that? And why? It's not exactly America's favorite pastime.

And is she doing something to her wrists? That is a nasty scar. I've heard about people cutting themselves. Maybe she has a brother who drives her crazy too.

"Zachary Berger! Are you there?" It's Mr. Piper.

Huh? I jump and everyone laughs.

"Zach, I've called on you three times, and I don't think the answer is on the back of Grace's head that you've been staring at for the last few minutes." More laughter as heat crawls up my neck.

He repeats the question about the difference between a ray and diameter of a circle, and I get it right. Math is easy, when my mind is on it.

• • •

The whistle-command quiz in archery is a breeze. Braden didn't have to take it. Everyone else, except Rudy Daley, gets 100%.

We all enjoy watching Rudy do his 50 push-ups. Rudy likes attention. He probably got one of the quiz questions wrong on purpose. His wavy red hair, freckles, and round belly belong in a TV commercial for hot dogs. Kids love him, but teachers think he's a smart aleck.

After 35 push-ups, I kind of feel sorry for Rudy. He's hurting.

Bart yells, "Better lay off those triple bypass burgers, Rudy!"

Everyone laughs, except Puddles. He's probably thinking the same about himself.

• • •

In the second week of archery Grace and I aren't exactly talking up a storm, but I compliment her on her rounds, and once she actually says "nice try" when I hit the second ring from the bullseye. When I whiff a shot, I hear her giggle. For some reason her laughter makes me all warm inside. Up until now, she acted like there was some grand prize on the line. So maybe she finally gets it: this is just gym class.

In the third week Grace is gone for four days in a row, which is strange. I mean, it's the last week of archery with a test tomorrow. I pace my bedroom talking in my head to Sam. Where is she? Did she move again? When did I start worrying about this girl more than about Braden? Sam is laughing over this.

• • •

Grace returns but offers no excuse as to why she was gone. She looks a mess. Her bright eyes are dull, and her usual smooth hair is a tangled nest. Even I can tell it needs brushing. She has bruises on one of her arms, and she only hits the bullseye once for the skills test.

"Have you been sick?"

Grace tenses and looks at me with dark guarded eyes.

What? I'm just trying to be nice and ask a simple question. You know, for conversation.

She shakes her head. Her face turns cloudy and she turns away.

Should I ask?

"You okay?"

No response. She's gripping the bow tightly and biting her lip.

Maybe I'll change the subject.

"I thought maybe I'd improve my shooting game while you were gone. Ya know, when you're not here staring me down." I make sure I say this like I'm kidding. "But as you can see I'm still a lousy shot."

"You just need practice."

Whoa. A whole sentence.

She steps right in front of me. As she leans in close and meets my eyes, I can feel her breath on my face. "And I'm not staring you down."

Oh.

Her eyes soften as she turns away but not before my face heats up. What's with all this blushing stuff? I don't remember this happening in sixth grade.

I look away and scream as the arrow Braden shoots sails into my leg. Thankfully it only nicks my thigh.

• • •

"I wanted to take the archery test," I hear Braden's explanation to Dad through the heating vent. Does he even realize he shot his brother?

I hadn't heard from Sam in a while, but I hear him loud and clear tonight. "Zach, I might start calling you Ponyboy. It's a dangerous world out there!"

Everything is fine.
–Zach

At the end of September, Nicotine Nancy will give us a quiz on *The Outsiders*, so the Phin-man and I get together to study at his house.

"Phinney, do you think there are kids in Hazard with problems like Ponyboy and Sodapop?"

"Oh sure. I think I saw a couple gangsters in Central Park last night."

"No, I'm serious."

"Since when do you get all worked up about stuff in a book?"

"I don't know. I think I have it bad with the weird stuff Braden does and two sisters that drive me crazy. But, no parents? Man, what would I do if something happened to them?"

"I bet Mad Marlys would take you in!"

"Oh, now there's a cheery thought. I'd rather live in

a ditch."

Later in my own room, I stare at my worn copy of *The Outsiders* and think maybe life is pretty good right now. No recent Braden disaster other than being shot with his arrow. Football, Sam, Phinney—all good.

I open to chapter nine. Tears fill my eyes as I read Johnny's words to Ponyboy to stay gold. The last line of Robert Frost's poem eats at me. *Nothing gold can stay.* Is that how life works? Things are good. Until they aren't.

I copy the poem onto a piece of notebook paper and push-pin it to my bulletin board. The effort exhausts me.

• • •

Only a few weeks into school and Bart and Monica are an item, which figures. Monica is way out of my league. Plus, my grades aren't exactly honor roll status, so I can't let distractions like Model Monica pull me off course. I need decent grades to stay in football.

Miss Thompson's after-school tutoring not only helps my science grade but my spirits. I only stay for fifteen minutes as football practice is right after school, and Coach Cole doesn't tolerate tardiness. Miss Thompson is so nice and (did I mention?) pretty. Even though she's probably over twenty-five, she wears lacy skirts and things that don't make her look like a teacher.

"Zach, I think you understand science. You just need to be more confident and realize how much you've got going for you. What do you think?"

I shrug. I can't tell her that this tutoring time is just part of my escape plan from Braden.

"Zach." I don't know why, but every time she says my name, I feel like I'm crumbling. "How is it to be in the same school with your brother this year?"

Which one?

"It's fine." It's barely a whisper and my throat feels tight.

I've sunk to using my parent's favorite line that is so far from the truth. What I feel like saying is, 'I wouldn't wish an autistic brother on my worst enemy.'

"It can be hard to have a sibling who has extra challenges. You are handling it well."

Not really.

I tighten my hands into fists on my lap and feel the heat moving up my neck and face, threatening my eyes. I feel like hitting something. Instead I hop up and announce, "I gotta go."

As I grab my backpack, she says, "It can't be easy." I

feel my armor cracking.

Her words light a flame to the gas can. I turn toward her and fire off, "I'm not looking for easy! I'm looking for normal."

I instantly regret this. What is wrong with me? First Mom and now I'm shouting at Miss Thompson.

"He's back, isn't he?"

I feel the world tip.

She obviously knows the answer so I don't bother replying. Maybe I don't need help in science anymore. No matter how nice it is to spend some time with Miss Thompson, I do not want to talk about my make-believe brother with her again—ever.

I decided to go back to teaching science.
Being a social worker was so
emotionally draining for me.
—Miss Thompson

I lay in my bed staring at the reflection of the moon on the wall. My alarm clock reads 2:31 a.m. I've been in and out of restless sleep since 10 p.m.

I try to think about normal stuff. Braden's got his bike back in one piece. Mom got her sofa and carpet cleaned. Dad's motorcycle is sitting on the curb with a "for sale" sign on it. I guess my allowance didn't quite cover the cleaning bill.

But then not-so-normal stuff drifts into my head. I can't get Miss Thompson's voice out of my head. *"He's back, isn't he?"* How does she always know what I'm thinking?

It all started in fourth grade. I was delivering a book to Miss Thompson for my teacher. She wasn't in her office so I sat and waited. I looked around at her posters and stuff on her wall and thought about the troublemakers she dealt with as a social worker.

Sam had already been with me for a while. Since I was alone in her office, I started having a conversation with him. Suddenly I saw Miss Thompson in the doorway. I don't know how long she'd been standing there, but long enough.

I spent half an hour every Monday for the next two years telling Miss Thompson about this crazy idea of fabricating a pretend brother named Sam and why I needed him. She wanted to tell my parents, but I begged her not to. I was afraid they would send Braden away—or me.

I remember her saying things like, "Many people have imaginary friends. Often they are young children with vivid imaginations. In your case, Zach, it's your way of dealing with Braden." She told me not to worry. That she knew I realized Sam wasn't real.

I'm pretty sure she thought I was nuts.

She said I'd someday see Braden was a fine brother, and I wouldn't need Sam and he'd go away. That hurt because I needed Sam.

"Why do you call him Sam?" Miss Thompson has asked.

"It's short for something." I didn't really want to tell her. "SUPER-Bro. And. Me."

Sometimes I didn't know what to think when Miss Thompson and I spent those Mondays talking about Sam. Of course he wasn't real, but the need to have a normal brother was. An older brother would share a bunk bed with me and teach me everything about every sport, or at least the important ones, like baseball and football.

Last year, when Braden was in the middle school and I was still at the elementary school, I had somewhat weaned myself away from having Sam. But Miss Thompson is right. Now that I'm in the same school as Braden again, Sam's back.

20

Who is Sam? I hear Zachary
talking to him in his room.
—Braden

Sunday night, Phinney comes over for pizza. We head to the basement for some gaming. Braden is down there organizing his stickers.

"Hey, Braden Buddy!" Phinney is cool with Braden.

Without looking up from his stickers, Braden mutters, "Zachary says you dress like a turd."

"WHAT?!" In unison Phinney and I respond.

"Braden, I said nerd, not turd." Braden acts like he didn't hear me, and Phinney just laughs.

"How was your date?" Phinney asks me as we settle onto the sofa.

"Huh?"

"Is she willing to wait for you?" Phinney is concentrating on the basketball video game we are playing.

When I figure out Phinney is talking about Miss Thompson, I throw a pillow at him. Hard. He unleashes his crazy laugh, and I end up laughing too.

The next morning I feel like something the cat dragged in, to quote my father. More nightmares. The worst one was about creepy robot babies that took over the world when they ate too many desserts. They had flapping hands and slept with their green eyes open. I tried hitting them with my bow but kept missing.

I wish I could stay home from school and sleep, but I'm afraid I'll fall behind. I have to keep my grades up to stay eligible for sports. Mad Marlys doesn't care what you do in study hall, so I try catching up on sleep there.

Middle school is a lot of work. I get a midterm warning in English and social studies because I didn't turn in some assignments. When I find out, I race home from school to check the mailbox. When I see the pink slips, I rip them to shreds so my parents won't see them, then tear back to school for football practice.

There's always a calm before the storm.
—Zach

"Braden seems to be behaving himself so far this year." Dad scoops another spoonful of cereal into his mouth.

It's almost the middle of October, and my stomach is in its usual morning knots. Mom insists breakfast is the most important meal, so I slowly pick at my bagel. "There's always a calm before the storm, Dad."

Dad has all these sayings like "if the shoe fits" or something is on "its last leg." But his favorite is "there's always a calm before the storm," which freaks Braden out since he hates storms. Once last summer when Dad used that line, Braden went berserk and holed himself up in the basement bathtub for hours because he thought we were all going to get blown away. When he finally came out, Carly told him it was raining cats and dogs which sent Braden right back to his tub sanctuary.

I hope there isn't a storm brewing with Braden. I

haven't thought about having to transfer schools since the first day when Braden nearly got pancaked by a bus, and Monica the Magnificent donned her Italian-flavored outfit.

I feel Dad's eyes on me. "How's football going?"

"Fantastic!" It's not often Dad inquires about my sports.

"Does your hair fit into your helmet?" Eva giggles her question at me. I've never had my hair this long.

"Why can't girls play football?" whines Carly.

"Because twerps like you would drive the coach crazy!" I swat her head as I get up to leave.

"I think it's a dumb sport," says Eva. "You get hurt."

"Football isn't dumb. It's the best part of middle school so far! Hey, Dad! Coach told me I have great hands." I find myself fantasizing about making a winning touchdown catch and having Dad actually be there to witness it.

"Great! Then use those great hands and take out the garbage." So much for trying to get Dad all excited about my athletic skills.

Practices have been boiling hot, but it feels satisfying to sweat after sitting at a desk all day. We've had two games with teams from neighboring towns, but today we are scrimmaging the eighth graders. This is always a great rivalry, and families come to watch. The eighth graders expect to win and have been trash talking us all week. We want to cream them, but of course, it's never been done.

I see my family on the sidelines. They even brought Hank and Beulah. Carly and Eva each have a leash and are running around. Someone stops to give Hank a bite of a hot dog. That will look swell on Mom's white sofa when he pukes it up.

I see Braden sitting on the bleachers in a Superman shirt all by himself. Sadness moves through me. I visualize Sam sitting there instead of Braden. He is calling out to pump me up. I notice the other guys getting into formation for warm-ups. I tell myself I better stay focused, or Coach won't play me.

As Coach leads us through pass and catch drills, I notice the eighth graders warming up on the south end of the field. They are bigger than us, but we have some fast guys. Maybe we can outrun them, if we could ever hold onto the ball. "This team has a bad case of fumble-itis," Coach yelled at practice one day. "The cure is practice, practice, practice!"

Braden is still sitting alone. Isn't there one person in this school who will sit by him? We win the toss and choose to receive. The eighth-grade kicker, Rusty Edwards, sends the ball sailing end-over-end down the field. Anthony Laine attempts to catch it but fumbles. He apparently hasn't been practicing.

He manages to pick it up and scrambles to the thirty-five yard line. Bart is our quarterback of course.

I start in as receiver, but seventh-grade football isn't much of a passing game. The first three plays are on the ground and don't get us the ten yards we need for a first down, so we punt the ball away. I don't usually play defense, since I'm not very big, but sometimes Coach has me at safety because of my speed.

On the third down, the eighth graders score with the quarterback running it in from about thirty yards. If I had been in as safety, I would have mowed him down to stop the touchdown run. He isn't that fast.

There are no goal posts on the practice field where we play, so they go for two points and don't get it. The score is 6-0.

On our next possession, running back Calvin Jaspers fumbles during a hand-off from Bart, and the eighth graders have the ball back. I guess Calvin needs practice too. They take advantage of our mistake and score again on a twenty-two yard touchdown pass. Another short pass into the end zone gives them two extra points, and we are down 14-zippo.

We have eight-minute quarters with a few water breaks scattered throughout. On our next set of downs, I hear Monica and her girl group cheering loudly but to no avail, as the game stands at 14-0 at halftime.

Coach Cole sends me in as safety at the beginning of the second half. The safety position is one that helps defend the pass play. The other team doesn't seem to be passing much either, but then they did get one score on a pass. Things are kind of back and forth evenly until the third quarter when Andre Dickson returns the ball sixty yards. I take him down 10 yards from the end zone.

The fourth quarter is pretty boring unless you count all the substitutions. Coach Cole follows through on his promise that everyone would get in the game. I am back in as a receiver.

With ten seconds left and the score still 14-0, we have the ball back. I am lining up right. The play will be a fake hand-off, and then Bart will look for an open receiver, probably Justin.

I glance to the sideline to establish my location on the field.

The field has a wall of tall pine trees on the west side that helps block the afternoon sun. Between two of the trees, in broad daylight, there is a boy with his back to the field peeing.

You have got to be kidding me.

I gasp. I don't know why I'm shocked. 'Par for the course' as my dad would say, when you have a brother like Braden who does embarrassing stuff every time you turn around.

Bart is calling signals. "Fifteen!"

I move my eyes desperately back and forth from the spectators to Braden. *Has anyone else noticed this? Is everyone blind today? I sure hope so.*

"Twenty-two!"

Still peeing! I can see the stream of water arcing toward the trees. He must have had a gallon of soda.

"Five!"

I panic when I see a bunch of younger boys running toward Braden, pointing and howling like a pack of wolves.

"Nineteen!"

The snap from center.

I scream at the top of my lungs. "Braden! Get behind the trees!"

Braden can't help but hear me. It's a mistake to have yelled at him though. He turns around and zips up his fly for the whole county to see.

Calm is done. The storm has arrived. Dad is right on the money.

The thundering sound of football players running jolts me from the awfulness. I propel myself forward from the line and turn toward Bart. I don't see the ball but I feel it. It makes solid contact with the top front of my helmet throwing my head back.

How in the world did it get to me that fast?

I watch the football spinning upward with the blue sky as its backdrop before gravity takes over. I spring up, snatch it, and land squarely on both feet.

I sprint forward into the end zone dragging a tackler with me and hear a thunderous cheer erupt from the sidelines.

We get the two extra points, and the final score is 14-8. Respectable loss, all things considered.

I butt helmets with Bart and get mauled by teammates but train my eyes on the trees. Braden is nowhere in sight, but I see the laughing boys near the trees and feel no joy about my touchdown.

I can hear Sam lecturing me already. "Braden's grass-watering trick will get around school in no time, and you'll both be the laugh of HMS." Or maybe he'd say, "It's Braden's problem, not yours. Be cool."

"We'll talk to Braden about appropriate places to pee," said Dad when I tattled. Good luck with that. All I can hope for is that those kids who saw him will not leak it to the whole school. No pun intended.

I wish Zach would stop asking so many questions.
—Grace

Archery is over, and we have had four days in a row of fitness testing. The fitness test consists of curl-ups, the sit and reach, push-ups, and the one-mile run. I am a strong athlete and look forward to this every year. Plus, exercise blows off a lot of stress.

The mile run takes us by the football practice field. "Hey Berger! After your brother peed on those trees, I'm surprised they aren't dying off by now."

If Bart has heard about this, the entire town of Hazard knows.

On Friday, the final scores of the fitness tests are posted. I have the third best boys score. Braden has the lowest. For the girls, Grace is number two, behind Abby Johnson who beat some of the boys in push-ups and the mile.

After the grueling week, I guess Puddles thinks we

deserve a break, so we fool around playing beanbag toss and suck on freeze pops. As we head back into school, Abby and Grace are in front of Phinney and me.

"Grace, you should try out for cross country with me."

Phinney agrees. "Yeah. First you wipe up in archery, and now you nearly knock off our number-one running girl!"

Grace laughs. "Actually, I *am* in cross country."

"No way! I've never seen you at practice," says Abby.

"Well, I do some volunteer work every day after school so I can't come to practice, but I run on my own."

This is the most I've ever heard her talk. Phinney and I stop at the door with Abby and Grace long enough for me to glance at her hands, but she's moved them behind her back.

"Where do you volunteer?"

Grace looks out of the corner of her eye at me. She acts like I'm grilling her every time I ask a simple question.

"At the homeless shelter."

Hazard has a homeless shelter? I didn't even know we had homeless people. Grace looks back at Abby and turns the conversation back to running. "Coach Gina says I can run in the meets as long as I have someone sign off on my practices."

I want to ask her who signs her practice sheets, but I'm sure she'd take that the wrong way.

"In fact, I'm running in Monday's meet!" Grace says with excitement.

"All right!" screams Abby, giving Grace a high five.

• • •

On Monday, Coach Cole lets us out of football fifteen minutes early. I slam my locker, grab my backpack, and sprint across the highway to the golf course. I had hoped to see Grace run in the cross-country meet today, but the school website showed the JV running at 3:45, so she'd be done by now. Maybe the Phin-man is over there and can let me know how she did.

The warm orange and yellow hues of autumn look like a painting, and I like the way they make me feel. I see a pack of varsity girls still running their race across the fairway. It takes me a minute to spot Phinney.

"How goes it?"

"Great! But it's a hot day to run. My meet is tomorrow, and I hope it cools off."

"Yeah, football practice was brutal today."

"How did Abby and Grace do?"

"Well, Abby pulled a muscle over the weekend so she's not running, and Grace didn't run JV."

She didn't show up. Why doesn't this surprise me?

"She's running varsity."

"No way! She qualified for the top seven?"

"I guess." Phinney checks his stopwatch. "The first runners should be coming up this hill in about two minutes."

I see runners stretched in a long trail along the backside of the golf course. There is a small pack of runners near the front, broken free from the rest and headed toward the last turn before climbing Heartbreak Hill.

I strain my eyes into the sun and look toward the top of the ridge. Spectators are yelling and cheering them on.

"Run! Dig in, Gina. Come on Kylie—get her."

The finish line is in front of us. Every time I watch these meets I can't believe it. Watching kids throw up and nearly pass out isn't my idea of a fun spectator sport.

The first runner to top the hill has a blue jersey and Decker High School printed across it. Decker is Hazard's big rival in everything. Someone named Alyssa Baxter. I heard this girl is expected to do well at state.

Close on her heels is Shontell Davis, our top runner

for Hazard. I don't recognize the next four as they're from other schools, but these first six girls are in a tight race. Once they top the hill they have a good 100 yards to the finish line. Each is straining and willing their bodies to finish the race before they collapse.

The Decker runner kicks it in for a strong finish. The pack is no longer tight but spread out, and it's clear the Decker girl has saved enough to take it home.

Another Hazard jersey has topped the hill. Girl Scout! *Unbelievable.*

"Well look at this!" Phinney says and starts screaming Grace's name.

Once on the flat, she picks up her speed, and she is smoking. Her body is erect, strong, and she has her eye on the finish line. With half the distance to go, she passes four runners, and the home crowd is screaming for her.

"RUN HAZARD, GO HAZARD!"

No one knows her name except Phinney and me, and I'm too stunned to speak.

"Kick it, Grace. Kick it!" Phinney has beat-boxed my eardrum.

She gains on Shontell, leans into the finish line and finishes a hair in front of her. The Decker runner wins but Grace is second! Unbelievable!

Coach Gina and Shontell run over and hug Grace. I feel an enormous sense of pride for her. I mean, new to town, running with the high school kids as a seventh-grader, and then taking the first team spot!

I follow Phinney over to Grace. She is walking off her run and breathing hard.

When she sees us she smiles and bursts into tears. But these are not the tears of a winner. Instead she looks broken. Before Phinney and I can figure out what to say, Grace turns and we let her go.

I really like it when Grace looks at me from only a foot away.
—Zach

Dance is our next unit in Phys. Ed. Mom is a whole lot more excited than me. "Hey, that means you and I can practice dancing. Your dad has never liked it."

"Mom, I don't like it either. This is for school, and the only reason I do it is because Pudd—I mean Mr. Presell is making us."

I could not picture Mr. Presell dancing, but he's surprisingly coordinated. He still sweats. A lot.

We watch a lot of dance-lesson videos to learn the steps, probably so Puddles doesn't have to demonstrate. We do the electric slide, the salsa, and even the polka, which my parents can't believe. Then we try fun ones like the shopping cart and, my favorite, the worm.

Dad can't stand the idea that we are using his tax dollars in school to learn a dance that impersonates someone putting items in a grocery cart.

Mom reminds him, as she is multitasking her way through making dinner, "When we were kids we learned disco in school. So what's the difference if he's learning the shopping cart?"

"The main difference is that we never admitted to our parents what kind of useless junk they were teaching us in school," insists Dad in an amused sort of way. "And I wasn't paying taxes back then!"

When we partner with a girl, we rotate so no one is stuck with one person for two weeks. I notice Braden has to dance with his teaching aide. If Sam were real, he wouldn't need an aide. He'd be the best dancer out here. He would...

My first partner, Maggie Martin, dances me back to reality. She takes charge and pretty much steers me around the gym floor. She spends the whole time asking me questions about Phinney.

"How long have you been friends?"

"Mmmm. A long time."

"Where does he live?"

"On Linden Street, by the water tower."

"What is his middle name?"

"I don't know."

"Can you ask him?"

"Maybe."

"Does he like any of the girls in our class?"

"Uh, maybe. We don't talk about that stuff."

"Yes you do."

What? Girls can read minds?

"Tell him I think he's cute."

Nerdman Phinney? Right-o.

Jennifer Bailey and I dance terribly together. She goes one way and I go the other, and we probably look like two robots with short circuits bumping around.

Next I partner with Abby. We laugh and exaggerate the steps to pretend we are on *Dancing With the Stars.*

When I rotate to Grace I anticipate a long, cold silence. I have been watching her dance with other boys and notice she's very stiff and stumbles a lot.

"Hi, Zach."

She said my name. Write that in the history book.

"Hey, Girl Scout."

No! I didn't just say that.

"What did you call me?" She squints at me. She looks accusing and amused at the same time.

The waltz music and Puddles' command save me from answering. "Grab your partner and remember, 1-2-3, 1-2-3."

"I'll explain later." What a moron I am.

"1-2-3, 1-2-3. Remember girls, right leg back, and slide, slide, left leg forward, and slide, slide, and repeat."

By now I am pretty decent at the waltz. But Grace isn't.

"Whoops! Sorry. Sorry!" She sounds so stressed. *Girl, it's just gym class!*

She trips now and then, and to prevent her from falling, I have to steady her by holding her tighter. I am enjoying her mistakes.

I have grown almost five inches over the past year and stand five feet, nine inches tall. Grace is a few inches shorter, so I watch her black lashes lying against her cheeks as she watches her steps on the floor.

"Man, I stink at dancing!" She stumbles again.

"So! Finally something I can do better than you!"

"A LOT better!" She looks up at me and, finally, laughs at herself.

I love her laugh. And I really like it when she looks at me from only a foot away. Several times we have to stop and restart. I review the steps with her so she knows what direction she should go.

Wait until Mom hears I taught someone to dance—a girl, even!

We finally give up and make up our own moves, which leaves us laughing. Once Grace steps on my untied shoelaces, and I fall.

"Wow, I need some serious help!" She giggles as she pulls me up.

"Maybe we can get together sometime, and I can teach you all I know about dancing," I tease.

"Sure! And then I can show you a thing or two about shooting an arrow straight!"

"It's a deal." And I hope she isn't kidding. "Where do you live?"

She goes silent. And she's back to her sullen self.

Mr. Presell stops the music to make an announcement.

"Before the bell rings I'm going to teach everyone one more dance called the Seventh Grade Special. It features Zach and Grace's signature dance move."

What? Everyone laughs, except Grace and me. Her face flushes deep pink, and I just shrug.

"It's called The Shoelace Step and goes like this..."
Oh man.

"I want all the boys to untie their shoelaces, and when I start the music, we'll see how long it takes the girls to step on the laces and make the boys fall."

I glance at Grace, and she is giggling with the best shade of pink in her cheeks.

People usually avoid me. But when we
play baseball, I am the all-time catcher.
–Braden

We live on a quiet street with no other kids in sight. I'm sure Mom and Dad planned that so Braden wouldn't bug them. His sensory system is on overload most of the time, and he doesn't need a bunch of crying babies or rowdy teens to rev him up. He seems to get there easily on his own. Storms, fireworks, my sisters' piano duets, even the furnace fans bother his ears. Too bad Grandpa Ben can't borrow one of Braden's eardrums. Grandpa can barely hear the person who is next to him, but I swear Braden can hear a raindrop fall in Ohio.

Our house is on a cul-de-sac so not a lot of people pass by.

I've decided that people with things to hide live on cul-de-sacs.

We recently got new next-door neighbors, the

Salzmanns. As soon as they moved in, they built an eight-foot fence around their yard. When they're not revving up a chainsaw, they spend a lot of time in a suspicious, little camper parked in front of their house. My guess is that they probably have a thing or two to hide. But then, we have Braden. Neighbors aren't always so excited to have a kid around who opens your mailbox to see if your junk mail contains stickers or stands in front of your house to count your windowpanes.

But there is one very cool thing about our neighborhood. It has its own baseball diamond behind the cul-de-sac, and whenever I can pull some friends together to play, it's a good time. Braden can't get the hang of baseball's rules, but he is our all-time catcher. He misses more balls than he catches, but he never minds chasing them down.

One hot fall Saturday, Braden stands up an hour into a game. "I need a break."

His timing stinks. As he stands, Kenny-the-Moose Anderson swings, and his bat connects with Braden's forehead. The head bleeds a lot.

Braden walks to me with blood gushing out of a nasty gouge near his hairline. In a voice as normal as if he's asking what time it is, he asks, "Z-Z-Zachary, am I still the all-time catcher?"

I take off my Joe Mauer t-shirt, wrap it around Braden's head, and steer him toward home.

Mom is in the middle of packing for our camping trip when we show up in the kitchen. "Zach, you need to get a haircut. You look like a—*Braden*! What happened?"

Braden never peeps. I wish he would scream or cry to let me know he actually feels something. Braden stares right into my eyes the whole way to the hospital while I hold the shirt tight on his head. I can probably count on one finger how many times he's done that, so it is a rare bonding moment. I wonder what he is thinking. I always wonder what he is thinking.

The ER is a lot more lenient than restaurants when it comes to letting you in without a shirt. I like breaking the rules once in a while, especially when Mom is around. They use that superglue stuff on Braden's head instead of stitches, since he goes nuts with needles. As they hold the two sides of his forehead together, my stomach flops, but I get to hold Braden's hand. He rarely lets me touch him.

Mom says, "We've been to the emergency room

five times with Braden. Maybe baseball isn't for him. We should just let him organize his keys and stickers. It's safer."

When I get home, I'll email Joe Mauer and let him know he was worth every penny he was paid, as his shirt saved my brother from bleeding to death. I wish there was a shirt that can save someone from autism.

I don't feel like going camping after that. I stare at Braden and wonder what river he'd drown in or what cliff he'd fall off. Braden had gotten so ripped off. What kind of a life is it with no friends and no way to keep safe? Other kids his age will soon have their driving permit. Dad said Braden would never learn to drive. That's the only thing worth living for when you're a boy. Well, that and sports. But Braden stinks at that too.

• • •

When we get home from the hospital, Dad is with my sisters. Even though they are identical, Braden and I have always been able to tell them apart. Carly has a feisty attitude and it shows even when she's talking in her sleep. "I wanna play baseball. I wanna play. I wanna play." She has zilch for patience and will not be the person to take care of Braden—ever!

Eva is a sweet, passive little thing who wants to care for every creature great and small in the universe. "Mommy, I'm going to have a butterfly house when I grow up, where people from all over the world can come and hold them." Good. Maybe *that* would be a safe place for Braden—in a butterfly house with Eva.

"Braden," Eva whispers when he gets home from the hospital. "How is your head? Do you want to watch your favorite show with us?"

"Yes. I w-w-want to watch the legislative session."

The day before, his "favorite" show was David Young playing Für Elise on a recorder on public television. Sometimes it's the local school board meetings. If he doesn't even understand how baseball works, I'm wondering what he's getting out of these shows.

Mom says his mind works differently than ours, and we can't compare him to us.

Spot on, Mom.

• • •

We spend nearly two hours loading the van with camping stuff, including the car carrier that goes on top. I used to love going to the cabin, but I always end up sharing a bed with Braden who insists on having four layers of blankets on. I push them off but somehow I find them back on me. By morning, I always feel like I've spent the night in a sauna.

"It's part of the whole sensory thing," Dad told me. "Being wrapped in heavy things gives Braden's body feedback and makes him feel more secure." Was I being selfish to think, 'What about me?' Does anyone give thought to what makes me feel secure?

We are all stuffed in the car waiting for Braden.

"Run up and get him, Zach," Dad says. "He was in your closet looking for something before I came down."

I fly out of the van. He better not be in my room!

He isn't. He isn't in any room or any closet or, we soon find out, anywhere in the neighborhood. After a two-hour hunt, Dad calls the police. A police dog goes into Braden's room and sniffs his clothes. His packed duffel bag stuffed with nothing but superhero shirts is on his bed. Beside it is the bandage that had covered his head injury. The dog sniffs that too. The police take a description and photo of Braden and ask a lot of questions.

"What if he has a concussion and he's blacked out somewhere?" Mom is a mess.

"Where will Braden sleep? Does he have food?" I have

never seen Carly so concerned.

For forty long hours, volunteers comb the town, the woods, and the fields. No one sleeps at our house. I spend the weekend thinking the worst.

When I was younger, there was no worrying; we were just brothers playing in the sandbox, pulling the dogs' tails, and wrecking our mattresses. I even used to help Braden line up his collections. Superheroes, army guys, millions of keys, and stickers. It got me out of a lot of chores. But where is he now? And who is going to watch out for him? I get ill thinking about that.

Sunday morning at 9:30, the police chief comes to our house to update us. No sign of Braden anywhere. He asks us more questions, plus some he had already asked. "Could he have stolen a car? Does he have a credit card? Does he know how to swim? Who are his friends? Is he dangerous? Suicidal?" Dad's eyes are red and puffy, and Mom can hardly speak. I have to leave.

I run to the garage and sit on the firewood box and kick at the bin of baseball equipment. Tears sting my eyes as I feel this sudden draw to Braden. I pull his catcher mitt out of the pile and put it on my hand. I hold it to my nose like the police dog, hoping I can catch a scent of

Braden, but all I can smell is musty leather. I pound my right fist into the glove and then hold it open, staring into the emptiness of it.

A baseball falls into the glove. I blink and it is still there. I hesitate before reaching out and touching it to see if it is real. Am I imagining baseballs too?

I jerk my head back and stare into the dark rafters. There he is sitting, his legs dangling down.

"I-I-I won't come down unless I can be aw-aw-all-time catcher again."

"Braden! What in the world? MOM! DAD!"

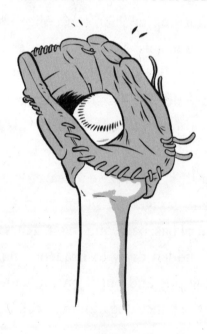

Sometimes I wish Zach would just chill out.
—Phinney

"So are you going to ask her out or what?"

I roll my eyes.

"Monica's taken, Phinney. I don't need Bart and his thugs beating me up."

"I wasn't talking about Monica." He stares at me with a grin. "You like her and you know it."

I don't know who the "her" is if he's not talking about Monica the Beautiful. I crease my brow and give him a questioning look.

"You really don't know who I am talking about? Well, here are two clues. She's the only pretty girl in seventh grade who got that way without an ounce of makeup, she stares at you every day as you leave math, and she can shoot an arrow with the accuracy of William Tell."

"That's three clues."

"Whatever. NOW you know who I mean."

"I'm not asking her out. I'm not asking anybody out." I kick a rock back and forth with Phinney as we walk home. "Plus, she's too…" I hunt for the right word. "Gloomy."

"Well, the winter dance is coming up and you could at least dance with her."

"She's a lousy dancer." I smile as I remember dance class.

"But you have your signature move you could do with her!"

I punch Phinney's shoulder until he convinces me to stop. Phinney. Sometimes he drives me nuts with his advice. It's like I have two mothers. It's not enough to have two brothers? And two sisters! Like Grace would come to a school dance anyway.

"I know who wants to go with *you* to the dance!" I tease Phinney.

"Miss Thompson?"

"Ha! Maggie Martin."

"What? How would you know that?"

"She told me to tell you she thinks you're *cute*."

"Right. You're making this up."

"Why would I do that? She told me when she was busy

dancing on my feet in Puddles' class."

Phinney's face glows beet red, something I've never seen. "So there's your date for the big dance, Phin-man! Don't say I never did anything for you. By the way, what's your middle name?"

"It's Gomer. Why?"

I laugh so hard I have to run to the bathroom to pee. Wait until I tell Maggie.

• • •

My social studies book is stuck. I wiggle it until it breaks free from the junk on the bottom of my locker.

"Is it later yet?" I turn and see Grace. I can't believe she actually walked up to me and is talking.

"Huh?"

I'm buying time.

"You told me you'd explain later."

I look confused even though I know exactly what she's asking.

"You called me Girl Scout. What's that all about?" I can't tell if she's mad or just curious. Or flirting? Okay, probably not that.

I pretend I'm still looking for something more in my locker, but she pushes it closed. And that's when I see them—bruises on her wrists. Just visible for a split second before her baggy shirt covers them.

Distracted by the bruises as well as her assertiveness, I tense and swing my backpack over my shoulder.

"It's no big deal." I shift my eyes from hers, which are way too close and aren't going to stop staring a hole through me until she gets an answer. A bunch of guys walk by.

"Practicing your signature move, Berger?"

"Hey, if it isn't the ol' Grace and Zach dancing duo!"

My face is warm. She isn't leaving. Time to fess up.

"Back on the first day of school, when you helped my brother clean up his tray and the floor? Well I was thinking you were like a... a Girl Scout. Ya know, doing a good deed and all that."

I sound stupid.

Somehow I manage to match her stare.

"Oh. Cool. And thanks for coming to my cross-country meet."

She turns to walk away, but I catch her arm. "Thank you for helping Braden when he dropped his lunch tray." My voice sounds thick and vulnerable.

Her eyes grow soft and watery as they meet mine. "It's

what we Girl Scouts do. We save people."

I get the feeling she isn't referring to Braden.

If people are mean to me, I usually don't catch on.
—Braden

"Hey, Girl Scout!"

I know I'm pressing my luck. She's wearing a baggy, long-sleeved shirt as usual so I can't see her arms.

Grace turns and waits for me to catch up with her. Pretending to be upset, she says, "I can't believe you just yelled that down the hallway for everyone to hear—Mr. Fred Astaire."

"Who?"

She rolls her eyes and says, "You don't know the most famous dancer of all time?"

"I guess not, but thanks for the compliment. And I thought that title belonged to Michael Jackson. Or Mr. Presell. "

Her eyes crinkle at the corners as she giggles. "Nevermind!" She's different today. Perky.

Grace stops at her locker to ditch her math book.

Before she closes it I notice a stash of granola bars, chips and juice boxes on the bottom of her locker. The kind we have in the cafeteria. *What is she hoarding all that for? Is there an approaching famine I didn't get the memo about?*

I don't want to ruin the moment, so I ignore the food and we head to the cafeteria. As usual I am starving. We collect a few stares, mostly from girls.

And here comes Phinney. He steps in front of us, forcing us to stop.

"I hope you two are ready for taco-licious Tuesday!" he says and then moves on with a wink.

"Phinney a close friend of yours?"

I smile. Now she sounds like Maggie.

"Sure is, the best money can buy. We're on a year-to-year contract though as BFFs, so I never know whether someone might steal him away."

Grace giggles, and I notice how smoothly she carries herself. Well, maybe not on the dance floor.

"Hey, remember the agreement we had in gym, how I would help you with dance if you teach me to get an arrow in the red zone?"

As she reaches for her tray she laughs at me, "I didn't say you'd ever get good enough to hit a bullseye."

She's making fun of me. Or is it just teasing? Where am I supposed to learn this stuff about girls?

"Well, I'm not sure someone who is as clumsy as you on the dance floor should be allowed to own and operate an assault weapon!"

She narrows her eyes and gives me an accusing look. "Very funny, Fred. Name the day and time and I'll be at your house for my first dance lesson."

Seriously?

"Is it okay if it's on the Wii and it's called 'Just Dance'?"

She throws her head back and laughs. "Lame!"

"How does this Saturday afternoon work?"

"Two o'clock?"

"Perfect!"

I notice the dessert police lady isn't on duty, so I take two desserts. I'm feeling lucky today.

We both go to our usual spots to eat—Grace with a couple of girls from our math class and me with the guys.

Did we just make a date? I can't stop smiling, and my school lunch never tasted better.

When she comes over to the house, I'll ask her about those bruises.

People talk about me and make decisions for me like I'm not in the room.
—Braden

I am so nervous about Grace coming to my house. The butterflies in my gut are working overtime. I'm afraid she'll cancel, but I am more petrified she'll actually show up.

I practice how I'll ask her about her bruises.

"What happened to your wrists?" Too direct.

"You look like you've been wearing handcuffs." Probably not the right way to go.

What advice would Sam give me?

It's 2:05. She's late. She'll call soon and tell me she had to volunteer at the homeless shelter. I feel relieved. Even though Grace seems more upbeat and actually talks to me, I wonder if it is short lived, that she'll retreat to her secretive self. *Nothing gold can stay.*

Grace told me she walks everywhere so I'm surprised

when I see her get out of the little transit bus. I watch her from my bedroom window. It is a cold December day so I'm glad she has a ride.

Maybe I should have asked my parents to pick her up? I'm new at all this.

I pace. Sam is feeding me advice. *Do not, under any circumstances, let Braden hang out with you when Grace is here.*

She walks with confidence up the driveway to the front door. Her gaze takes in the neighborhood. She stares next door at the Salzmanns' property longer than I would have liked her to. But who wouldn't? Five barking dogs and a security fence make the place look more like a prison yard than someone's home. She probably lives in one of those mini-palaces near the golf course.

Thankfully, Mom is not at home so she won't be grilling Grace. My mom's real estate work takes her out of the house a lot on weekends. Driving clients around and showing them property until they find their dream house takes a while.

"This is my Dad. Dad, this is Grace." This all feels awkward.

I can tell Dad is purposely holding back in the

question department. He probably had a mom like mine so he knows what it's like to be in my shoes. In fact when I think of Grandma Penny, I am positive of that. Every time she comes over, she quizzes us on everything from politics to clean underwear.

"Zach tells us you are quite the archery pro."

Grace smiles. "Well, he's quite the dancer so we thought we could help each other out." She's being humble.

"He also says you're a star runner on the varsity cross country team this year! You must come from a great running family." Dad's voice sounds impressed.

"My mom and I... we..." Her voice catches and suddenly she looks uncomfortable. "We used to run together."

As I follow Grace down our basement steps to our rec room, I suddenly feel self-conscious about dancing in front of her all by myself. Dancing in gym class is one thing. But now I'm sweating and wondering why we didn't go and shoot arrows instead. I excuse myself so I can put deodorant on.

By the time I return, the Carly and Eva Show has invaded. They are rocking with the dance video on the old TV, and Grace is right there with them. I watch for a second from the bottom of the stairs and feel this nice thing inside me. That doesn't happen to me much when I'm home. I feel calm.

"Come on, Fred!" giggles Eva. What? I'm gone for a minute and Grace has already shared her pet name for me? Eva pulls me over and wills me to dance. The four of us twist and spin and make up silly dance moves for nearly an hour. My sisters love to dance and sing, and since Grace has hit it off with them, I don't make Dad kick them out. Plus, they take the pressure off me.

It's a relief that the ancient TV is working today. I have tried talking Dad into getting a flat-screen, but then he goes off on his lecture about how his family used rabbit ears on their TV when he grew up and that you sure couldn't play video games on it (because there were no video games) and that the TV went off the air at midnight when the national anthem was played. That's when I tell him I love the idea of us still having a console from the 90s.

Braden comes down with his sunglasses on and stares at Grace for a long ten minutes.

Creepy.

But Grace doesn't seem to be bothered, and I don't

want to risk a Braden Bomb going off by asking him to leave.

After all our dance fun, we are exhausted and thirsty so I take Grace upstairs for something to drink. I grab the cookie jar and watch as Grace downs four or five. I guess she worked up an appetite! Maybe this is the right time to ask her about her bruises? How do I casually bring that up? Her sleeves cover her wrists as usual.

Carly and Eva come running in and grab cookies. They are still dancing and singing. Of course they are showing off for Grace, giggling and asking her if she wants to hear their piano duet, and telling her she has pretty hair.

Braden comes in and stares some more at Grace. He doesn't have his sunglasses on, but I wish he did because his staring is more obvious when he's not behind his shades.

"Do you have stickers?" he asks Grace. *Aw, geez.*

Grace nods, "A few."

"Can I have them?"

"Well, I don—"

I jump up and interrupt. "DAD! Braden needs you!" But Dad has gone to walk the dogs. Once again, the disappearing Dad act.

Braden shuts up and settles for staring at Grace instead of asking her for more stickers.

If autistic kids have so much trouble with eye contact, then why does Braden stare at people so much? I nudge Braden on the shoulder and mouth the words, "Stop staring." The flapping begins. Grace keeps looking at the cookies and doesn't seem to notice. Suddenly, Braden dashes out of the room and up the steps.

"Helloooo! I'm home!" It's Mom. "It is wonderful to finally meet the girl who is such an archery whiz! That's a bit of an unusual sport, especially for a girl."

Here we go with Mom's Interrogation 101.

Grace shrugs like it's no big deal. "Not really. I just like to learn things that I can actually use and not waste my time on silly things."

I can see the wrinkle crease between Mom's eyebrows before she takes up her line of questioning again.

"I see. And where did you learn how to shoot?"

"Dad taught me."

"Is there an archery range somewhere in Hazard?"

"Uh, I don't really know."

"So where do you practice?"

"We just set up our own targets."

136

"You mean like tin cans and that kind of thing?"

"Sort of." Grace's answers are getting shorter, and I'm wondering how to shut Mom down.

"Doesn't your mother think a bow and arrow is dangerous?"

Grace's eyes cloud over and there's an uncomfortable silence. I jump in to save her.

"Mom, Mr. Presell taught us archery safety. Grace, what did you think of the sub we had in math on Wednesday?"

Grace is quick. "She was okay. Some of the kids were mean to her though. I feel sorry for subs becau—"

"We need to go to the store." Braden is back carrying two large jars of stickers. "I don't have many stickers left."

Only two or three thousand, but who's counting?

"Braden, don't get all bent out of shape. You already have zillions of stickers," I say crossly. "And apologize to Grace for interrupting."

"I'm not bent. I'm a regular shaped boy."

Carly and Eva giggle.

"How many zeroes does zillion have in it?" Braden continues. "I didn't know I had a zillion stickers."

Mom casts a line to get Braden off the sticker train.

"Braden, has Zach introduced you to his friend?"

Peering into his jars of stickers, Braden flatly states, "I-I-I already know her. She cleaned up the mess I dumped all over that m-m-mean girl. I need more stickers."

"What did I miss?" Dad is back with the dogs.

"What mess?" Mom needs to know the gory details.

Naturally my parents turn to me for an explanation. I give them nothing other than a disgusted headshake. This is what my dating life is going to look like: one big miserable circus show with Braden as the ringleader.

"It was a long time ago and no big deal," Grace says, trying to let it slide.

"Hank is s-s-staring at Grace. Why can't I?" Braden asks.

"And what mean girl?" Mom pushes.

"Braden's talking about Monica, and Monica's pretty, Mom. Not mean." *Why did I just say that in front of Grace?*

"Monica is one of the hot chickens at the school," Braden says.

I nearly choke on my lemonade.

"Hot chickens!" Dad yells. Eva and Carly practically fall off their chair laughing.

Grace stifles a laugh and glances at me. This is not

funny to me.

I grit my teeth. "Braden dropped his lunch tray the first day of school."

"And?" Mom is wasting her time being a realtor. She'd make a killer detective.

"My spaghetti went all over that hot chicken's hair." Braden starts laughing so hard he is snorting. "And clothes." This time we all laugh uncontrollably. Even me.

I wonder why something can seem so awful when it first happens but later it's so hilarious that you laugh until your face hurts. Maybe it's because my laughing is really close to crying. Most Braden episodes affect me like that.

Mom tells Grace at least three times how nice it is that she helped Braden when he dropped his tray.

At 5 pm Grace stands up. "I need to go home."

I guess I won't learn about those bruises today.

"You can't stay for dinner?" Mom offers.

Grace eyes the counter where Mom has a pan of vegetarian lasagna prepped to put in the oven, as well as a store-bought apple pie. Grace gives a regretful headshake. If she only knew about Mom's cooking, she wouldn't look like she's missing something.

"Do you need a ride, sweetheart?"

Grace's face turns quickly toward Mom, and she looks startled, like she is going to cry. She blinks and whispers, "What did you just call me?"

"Um." Mom looks confused. "I just asked if we could drive you home?"

"No no, I can walk."

"It's getting dark and it's starting to snow. Where do you live?" *Excellent question, Mom.*

"Not far."

"Jason, why don't you drive her home? Zach can ride along."

"I can do that. But maybe she wants to walk." *Good ol' Dad.*

"You can drop me at the Elm Street gas station. Dad will be there."

"He works there?" Mom's tone makes it clear that she doesn't consider working at a service station a real career for a parent.

"Only on weekends. He's looking for a second job."

Mom's eyebrows shoot up, and I can only imagine what she's thinking.

The idea of meeting Grace's dad gives me an angry feeling in my gut, and my throat goes dry. Maybe I should ask *him* about those bruises on Grace's wrists.

I put a fistful of Mom's hard cookies into a bag and hand it to Grace before we head out. The way Grace smiles at me when I hand them to her—well, I'll give her cookies every day for that.

We pull up to the corner station. "There he is." Grace points to a tall guy changing a tire.

When Grace gets out of our car, her dad notices her and steps out of the garage, wiping his hands on a greasy rag. He approaches our car and I tense. His arms are muscular, and I find myself staring at his hands as he reaches in to shake hands with Dad. He has thick brown hair that looks more like a teenager's cut. His face surprises me. He looks young, but his shoulders sag and his eyes look tired.

He pulls Grace toward him. Like he owns her and isn't going to let her get away.

"It's a pleasure to meet you. I'm Greg Elliott." His voice is strong like his arms.

He turns to me.

"And you must be the Zach I've heard about." He crushes my hand with his vice-grip handshake. It wouldn't take much to leave a bruise with hands like that.

"Did you manage to teach Grace a few more dance moves?" I can't tell if he's accusing me of something or just making conversation.

"She did great." I try to sound normal.

"I'll expect a dance show when we go home," he says with an insistence that I don't like.

"I had fun, Dad."

Mr. Elliott tightens his grip on Grace's shoulder.

"Great. Well, thanks for driving her. I understand an archery lesson is up next!" He smiles, and I notice it's the same great smile as Grace's.

"That's what I hear," Dad says. "Grace, maybe your mom can call and reassure Zach's mother that shooting an arrow is a safe sport."

Grace's dad glances down at her with a questioning look. She gives him a tight smile and doesn't respond. Something's off. Other than my suspicions about her dad, I am feeling great about Grace's visit and feel like my whole body is smiling. Is this what it feels like to have a crush on a girl?

I can almost see Sam nod.

I want to text Grace to thank her for coming over, but I don't have her phone number. Even if I did, it would be dangerous to text my friends on Mom's phone. I can imagine her reaction if she were to get a text from Phinney asking me about my crush on Grace, or Miss Thompson!

I keep telling Zach, forget about Grace.
Go for Monica.
—Sam

In art class we are working on shading: dark gray, medium gray, light gray. I'm not much of an artist, but this isn't really drawing. Just shading. Boring, really. But I love this hour because we can move around and talk to anyone as long as we're working on our shading.

It's Thursday and Monica moves her paper and drawing pencils over to my desk, then pushes her chair close to mine. Way too close, actually. Our arms are touching.

What in the world is she doing?

"Who are you taking to the winter dance, Zachy?"

You. And after the dance, will you run off with me and get married? I bet you've always dreamed of marrying someone who has a brother who drops his drawers in public.

"I haven't really thought about it," I say.

She has on purple eye shadow and smells sweet, like peaches.

"What do you mean? It's only two weeks away!"

Why do I always sweat so badly around girls?

I concentrate on my darkest shade and go over and over it.

"I have an idea," she purrs. "You could ask me."

WHAT?

I practically gag on my own saliva. I move my eyes left and right, worried someone has overheard her.

Man, this girl's bold. I look right into those baby blues and stammer, "Wh-why aren't… How come?"

I sound like an idiot. After oxygen returns to my brain, I try again. "Why aren't you going with Bart?"

"He has to go to his cousin's wedding… and I'd rather go with you, anyway."

It's really hot in here.

"Serious?" my voice squeaks.

"Yes." And she nudges my elbow and giggles.

My heart is pounding so hard I swear the whole class can feel it hammering.

"Pick me up at 7:00." She moves her stuff back to her own desk, and the bell rings.

Unbelievable. I have a date with supermodel Monica Monahan. And knowing Monica, it's going to take approximately five minutes for this news to get around the school and back to Bart. He's gonna freak. I'll be a dead man. But a very happy dead man. Maybe it's finally payback time for the junk Bart did to Braden last summer.

I see Sam grinning from ear to ear.

Naturally, Monica tells everyone that *I* asked *her* to the dance. Bart blows a gasket.

So I use the line I'd heard in a movie once. "We're just going as friends, Bart." I want to set him straight that Monica asked *me*, but that might make him even more mad.

"If you were in town Bart, she'd be with you. Plus, I have to keep an eye on my brother at the dance. So how much time am I really gonna spend with your girlfriend?"

Never mind that Braden isn't even going to the dance.

"In fact, the way I see it, Bart: I'm doing you a favor keeping her away from all the other guys who will be lining up to dance with her while *you*, my man, are out of town."

I sound more confident than I feel.

"Berger. I'm gonna have my posse watching you and,

for your sake, I hope your 'friends' story holds up."

When I see Phinney later, he is beaming.

"Zach-man, you're going to the dance with Monica! Which magic man helped you pull that one off?"

I think the answer is Sam!

29

Zach has a perfect family. He is so lucky.
—Grace

I'd been saving my giant peanut butter jar of coins to buy something special. I wonder what Sam might suggest.

"Hey! Why don't you get some binoculars so you and Braden can spy on the weirdos next door?" Yes, a big brother would have such creative ideas. Ugh! I can't believe I am back to having conversations with my fake brother.

I am surprised when the bank teller tells me I have $48.45 in the jar. "Congratulations on disciplining yourself to save your money. What are you planning to do with it?"

Braden is beside me and blurts out the truth, "We're going to get binoculars to check out hot chickens."

My ears grow hot, but the teller just giggles.

Braden has never used binoculars before. I help him adjust them, and he looks at the stars, the neighbors' doorknobs, and the Salzmanns. He loves this. We find a gap in the tall fence about an inch square. Only one of the binocular lenses fits up against it, but it's enough to give us a glimpse of part of their backyard. It's a boring part where they park their riding lawn mower. But beside it, there's a huge hole with a big hunk of wood, about eight feet tall, stuck in it.

The other thing we see through that hole is their beast of a dog chained to a stake. The next day, we hear the chainsaw and run to look through the hole, but it's been covered with a metal piece from the other side.

But for weeks, I do notice people coming and going from the Salzmanns'. They pull up in shady-looking converted vans and loud motorcycles. Some stay. Others meet the old guy in the driveway, and they exchange something through their car window before they leave.

One day, a guy pushing a younger man in a wheelchair catches my attention. He heads right to the Salzmanns' padlocked gate, taps a code into a keypad, and pushes the gate open. They disappear into the garage, and the gate closes. An hour later, the man who had been pushing the wheelchair drives a shiny new car out of the garage and leaves.

Mom catches me spying and blah-blah-blahs about how I should use my time more wisely by emptying the dishwasher. So I empty the dishwasher, but when Mom leaves to buy groceries, I return to my perch in the dining room. The wheelchair dude and the oldest Salzmann son, Randall, have come out of the house. It looks like the guy in the wheelchair doesn't have any legs. He's holding something that looks like a wine bottle in one hand and hands an envelope to Randall with the other. I open the window to see if I can hear them.

They pass by the flea-bitten dog and go to the camper. Randall lifts the man in the wheelchair up and into the camper. Soon, I hear muffled shouting and swear I can see the camper rock.

WHAM!

What was that?

When I hear the bang again, I realize it is coming from our back door.

WHAM! WHAM! Geez. Hold on. Did Braden lock himself out again?

I run to the door with my binoculars still in my hand. I open it to find the bearded Mr. Salzmann staring me down. I gasp. An old camouflaged cap is pulled tight on his head, leaving some gray and brown hair sticking out. He is a lot taller than he looks through my binoculars. Dirtier, too. And what is he hiding behind his back?

I want to move back, but I feel paralyzed. Part of Mr. Salzmann's jaw and cheek are missing. The whole left side of his face is grotesquely sunken and discolored, and his left ear is gone. This is one guy who looks better from a distance.

The old man slowly moves his arms out from behind his back. I sway at the sight of his chainsaw.

SAM!

I like seeing those kids next door.
—Mr. Salzmann

I stumble back. My mouth feels like sandpaper.

"What do you want?" I croak.

He is staring at my binoculars, and I quickly move them behind my back. I wonder if he has caught me spying and has come to take care of the problem. My mind is racing through all the ways he could do that. Starting with that chainsaw.

I push the binoculars stiffly out toward his face. "Here. You can have 'em."

Raising his chainsaw in front of my face, he speaks. "That ain't what I came for."

His voice is surprisingly quiet and calm. His smoky breath drifts toward me, and I'm estimating it's been a couple months since he's brushed his teeth. Not that he has many to brush.

He's not satisfied to take my spying tool; he's come

to take me out. Maybe he thinks I've seen too much. My knees feel like Jell-O, and I need to pee in the worst way.

"I need to use your phone," he says, even softer than before.

Huh? You mean before or after you kill me?

"I'm not supposed to let strangers into the house when my parents are gone." My heart is still pounding so hard he has to hear it.

"Your parents are gone?" he says dryly. I swear I see a smirk tug at the corner of his mouth.

Why in the world would I say that? "Uh, they'll be back in a few seconds." I squeak. "Can you come back then? Or better yet, I'll have them call you."

"They ain't gonna call me. My phone's out."

Oh. Right.

Hasn't this guy ever heard of cell phones? He's got all those fancy expensive toys, and he's trying to tell me he doesn't own a cell? Somehow I don't believe him.

And then there's the chainsaw. He sees me staring at it.

"It's an emergency. I need a phone." There's silence as he stares a hole through me. "Please."

Oh, a polite criminal.

"And I'm *not* a stranger." He looks accusingly at my binoculars as he states this.

I motion stiffly toward the last rotary wall phone in the world. As he moves toward it, I back away and rush out through the door, gulping in the afternoon air.

I'm almost 13. Sam's gotta go.
—Zach

"My favorite time of the year is finally here, Mom!" I throw the basketball to her as she walks through the living room.

She catches it. "Fine Zach. But just remember, it's never basketball season in our living room."

Oh Mom, lighten up.

"Mr. Piper is the coach, and the rumor is if you do well in his math class, which I do, that you have a decent chance of getting playing time. I do not want to spend the whole season on the bench."

After those midterm warnings, I've managed to pull my grades up enough to remain eligible for sports, but my parents aren't impressed with them. Three Cs, a B-, a B+ from Puddles, and an A- in math.

• • •

Coach Piper starts our basketball practices with his

famous speed drills, where we have to sprint up and down the court. Then we do shuffling drills, where we race back and forth so long and hard I am dripping wet.

"The winning team is the one that can outrun the other team," he shouts repeatedly and makes us echo his mantra.

We don't do much weight lifting. Seventh graders are at the bottom of the pecking order when it comes to the weight room. And it ticks Coach off.

"How do they expect to raise up a state champion varsity team if you don't put muscles on the player early?"

So he dreams up Plan B: rope-zilla. Coach hands us a jump rope and blows his whistle long and hard. We start jumping. When he gets around to blowing it again, we have to drop and give him ten push-ups, then it's back to jumping rope. This goes on until our legs and arms drop off, or our chests incinerate.

"Why do we jump?" he yells.

"For agility, quickness, and stamina!" we shout in unison.

Someone said he was in the Army for twelve years before he got to Hazard. It explains a lot.

Basketball works my body and my brain so there's no

time to worry about Braden. A reassuring Sam watches from the bleachers.

I'm almost 13. Sam's gotta go.

That Zach Berger is so out of it lately.
He must be lovesick.
—Mr. Piper

Between school, basketball, and the usual chaos at home, the days sail by. Some mornings I'm so exhausted I can hardly drag myself out of bed. But on the plus side, I have a date with Monica for the school dance!

"Braden, you should go to the dance. You love to dance!" Mom insists.

"I'm not g-g-going."

Thank goodness.

I do everything I can to hide my excitement over my first date with the most popular girl in seventh grade, and I don't tell my family. I don't need the momma drama.

I do worry about dancing, though. I hope there aren't any slow dances, as that's just too weird for me to think about.

Two days before the dance, Carly and Eva tear up the

steps and through the door of my bedroom, chanting, "Zachy's got a girlfriend, Zachy's got a girlfriend."

They prance around me and sing their chant, over and over, until I chase them both out. They giggle and continue their chant down the hall.

Somehow Monica's gossip zip line has reached my second-grade sisters. Now I have to figure out how to bribe them to keep their traps shut so my parents don't find out. I don't need them lecturing me on girl stuff.

"Zachary Jason Berger, why didn't you tell us you asked a girl to the school dance?" Mom asks as she sets out the cereal boxes and bowls.

I groan and shoot daggers at my sisters as I sit down for another breakfast I have to gag down.

"Why can't you two mind your own business?"

"Oh, it wasn't them. Braden told us. He says she is very pretty."

Braden enters the kitchen and sits on the other side of the table. I give him a nasty look, but he doesn't have a clue what that means, so I'm wasting my time.

"Her name is M o n i c a." Carly exaggerates Monica's name like she is introducing a movie star.

"What's her last name?" Mom asks.

Next she'll want to know her parents' names, what they do for a living, and whether Monica gets stellar grades.

"Monroe," Braden answers.

I give Braden the *OHMYGOD-I-don't-think-so!* look and choke down a spoonful of cereal.

"Hmmm... Monica Monroe. I don't think I've heard of her. Is she new to town? What are her parents' names?"

No one answers. Finally I say, "I don't know, but I think her sister is Marilyn."

Mom laughs. The rest don't get it.

"She's the hot chicken I spilled spaghetti on," Braden states.

"Braden!" I shout.

"The mean one?" Of course Carly would remember this.

Always the one to try and smooth things over, Eva sweetly says, "Well, she must have liked it since she's Zachy's girlfriend now."

"She is *not* my girlfriend. I didn't ask her to the dance. She asked me. And it's Monica *Monahan*, not Monroe!" I shove my chair back and stomp out.

I grab my backpack and bolt out the door. Braden

can figure out how to get to school on his own. I don't care how many buses run him over.

Monroe! Where the heck did he pull that one from?

I don't know why I'm so mad. But I think Grace has something to do with it. I could kick myself for not asking her to the dance.

Grace is full of surprises.
—Zach

"When do you want your lesson?"

Grace turns around and talks to me at the beginning of math now. She isn't the real talkative type, but her voice is soft and she says only what she has to. Most girls I know are drama queens and talk and talk. Sometimes I wish their lips would just freeze up. But I like Grace's lips.

Today Grace has on a gray and blue sweater that hangs down past her hips. The sleeves are rolled up a couple times but still cover her wrists. I don't spend much time scoping out girls' clothes, but it seems like a lot of Grace's clothes are too big for her. Maybe that's the new look.

"Lesson? Are you kidding? It's winter and we have two feet of snow. If I shot an arrow you'd never find it until spring."

She giggles, which makes her eyes twinkle. "First of

all, we hardly have any snow on the ground and second, you're not going to miss the target once you get a lesson from me!" She sounds completely confident of this.

"Oh, I see. You're going to reverse three weeks of Puddles' instruction, which I apparently flunked, in one fell swoop."

"Yep!"

"I wouldn't bet on that. In fact, if you can get me to hit even one bullseye at your place, I'll..."

"Take me to a movie?"

What? This girl is full of surprises.

I laugh. "Oh, I get it. You have ulterior motives for teaching me how to shoot."

"With popcorn?" She is looking out of the corner of her eye at me and waiting for my answer.

I guess the girls make the dates in this school.

"And *extra* large popcorn with a drink?"

"Now you're getting greedy."

"No. Just making sure you really want to learn how to shoot better."

I want to tell her I don't give a rip about archery. I just want to spend time with her.

"I can come over Sunday, but I don't know where

you live."

I have asked her twice where she lives. First she said she was moving and then it was "near Manley Wood." That's definitely not near the golf course, so maybe her house is a palace on a country estate.

"I can bike to your place," I say.

"You bike in the winter?"

"Yep. My bike has fat tires to grip snow." But thinking about biking or doing any activity lately tires me out.

"You know where the blue water tower is?" she asks. "Meet me there at 1:00, and we can walk to where I keep my bow."

She has a *place* where she keeps her bow.

"Wait a sec. I have to volunteer this weekend," she remembers. "How about a week from Sunday? Zach?"

"Yea. Oh, sorry. Yea. Next Sunday works." My head feels woozy.

"Are you alright?

"I'm fine." The Berger mantra.

• • •

I bike to Grandma and Grandpa's house to try to beat Grandma in double solitaire.

"Grandma, did you ever make a decision you regretted?"

She laughs. "Only about every day!"

"Zachary, what is the matter?" Grandma asks. "You look pale."

I wonder how many months it's been since I've had a full night's sleep. If Grandma is noticing, I must really look bad.

"Here, have a cookie. And remember Zachary, regret is a waste of time. Saying you're sorry isn't."

I can't believe Zach took Monica to
the dance. I thought he liked me.
—Grace

Should I wear the same shirt to the dance that I wore all day in school—my plaid blue one with that stuffed-in-my-drawer wrinkled look? Am I supposed to look like I'm working at impressing Monica? There must be books on this stuff, like *Middle School Dressing for Dummies*.

I pull on some nice khakis and a different shirt with the same wrinkled look. And deodorant. Lots.

I was excited about the dance but feel on edge for some reason. Mom breaks the news to me that she talked Braden into going. She must have promised him a boatload of new stickers if he went. I have no energy to argue with her about it.

At 7 pm sharp, Dad drives me to Monica's house to pick her up. When she comes downstairs, she does resemble Marilyn Monroe with all that makeup and blonde hair.

Dad winks at me when he drops the three of us off at the front door of the middle school. Yes, Braden is with us. Arguing about this with Mom was a waste.

Puddles and Nicotine Nancy are serving as security. Phinney and Maggie meet us at the door. I look at Phinney's clothes. "What in the world…?" He gives me a tip of his safari hat and grins. I laugh and feel my blood pressure coming down a notch.

As I'm hanging up our coats, I can't believe it's me that Monica has chosen as her stand-in for Bart. I look at her as she walks toward the gym. It seems she's had another trip to the mall. She's wearing a tight lace overlay thing over a black mini dress. Does she realize we're in a little Indiana town, not Hollywood? I don't think she's even looked at *my* clothes, which is probably a good thing.

Sam interrupts my thoughts. "This is your chance, my man. Don't blow this."

I glance around and wonder where Braden is. Probably still at the entrance.

Monica grabs my arm and pulls me into the gym. When I see her Hollywood red-lipped smile, I am no longer Braden's brother. I'm Brad Pitt. Or maybe

Justin Bieber.

It's dark except for the exit lights and the D.J. equipment. The flashing of a strobe light disorients me for a minute. A twirling mirrored ball hung from the ceiling, along with some pulsating music, has transformed Mr. Presell's gym into a dance club.

It takes a while for my eyes to adjust. I look around and see Miss Thompson in the corner.

The D.J. is playing Katy Perry's "Firework." Monica drags me onto the dance floor where everyone is singing along.

Do you ever feel/ Like a plastic bag
Drifting through the wind/ Wanting to start again
Do you ever feel/ Feel so paper thin
Like a house of cards/ One blow from caving in

I feel like the questions in the song lyrics are for me.

There's a big crowd on the dance floor, and Phinney is the center of attention. He's dressed as part safari hunter, part leopard, and dances like a wild animal that's just been let out of a cage. He pounces toward other kids and roars and makes a scratching motion with his arms, causing everyone else to roar.

"Play the Macarena!" someone yells. The D.J. obliges. Puddles joins us and that guy is smooth. Other teachers get into it too. Mad Marlys may be old, but she can still move it!

After nearly an hour we take a break. Monica runs off to the girls' room with a half dozen of her fan club, and I head to the cafeteria with Phinney.

"Phin-man, you look like you robbed the Goodwill store!"

"I call it chick-magnet!" he says, and I laugh with him.

I look around and can't believe how many people are here. Phinney and I have a soda, and I find myself smiling, until I turn around.

Braden is sitting at a table by himself on the other side of the cafeteria. My heart sinks. Should I pretend I don't see him? But he's probably been sitting there all night alone. I should go over and talk to him.

Don't do it. He's not your problem.

I feel instantly guilty for all the fun I've been having.

You're gonna blow it with Monica if you go over there.

Phinney yells, "Zach-man, I'm heading back to the gym. I gotta teach those girls more of my moves!" I give him the thumbs up before I turn toward Braden.

A girl has just sat down and is talking to him. I can only see the back of her but I'd know that hair from a mile away.

My stomach dips and my heart starts pounding. Grace is here! She hasn't spoken to me since finding out I was going to the dance with Monica. She gets up and goes to the concession stand. I've never seen her in a dress, and it actually looks like it's her size.

I slowly move toward them, curious. I've never seen Braden with a girl before. She has bought Braden a couple slices of pepperoni pizza—his favorite—and an orange Crush, the only soda he'll drink.

When I get to their table they are laughing over something. I'm glad to hear she still finds something to laugh about.

"Hey Braden! Having some pizza?"

"S-s-starving. My friend and I are eating." Braden takes a huge bite, leaving pizza sauce all over his mouth.

"Hi, Grace," I try to sound friendly. She's not buying it. She picks up her pizza and completely ignores me. I deserve this, but it bothers me that she won't look at me. I notice her long lashes. "Can you believe how packed this place is?"

I'm trying real hard here, Grace. Help me out.

Why do I feel like a hypocrite? Because I've left Braden alone for Grace to save? Or that I'm here with Monica instead of her? I sit down beside Braden.

Sam is yapping in my ear. *"Why did you just sit down there? Monica's waiting."* Easy for him to say.

Grace is obviously angry and not talking. Maybe I should leave and let her go back to entertaining Braden.

An arm wraps around my neck. "There you are, Zachy! Are you gonna buy me something to drink? All that dancing with you has made me *so* thirsty!" Monica and company have surrounded me with loud, annoying giggles.

Embarrassed, I stand up. "Uh, sure."

"Well hello, Gretchen," Monica says to Grace, laying the sappiness on way too thick. "What in the world are *you* doing here?"

Grace rears back in her chair and is about to attack, but I get there first.

"Her name's Grace."

Monica doesn't even register that, but continues, "Don't you have something better to do tonight—like squirrel hunting with your bow and arrow?"

Oh boy. Mean girl.

"You're that hot chicken I dropped my spaghetti on."

OHMYGOD. Braden buddy, tell me you did not just say that.

I dare a glance up at Monica. If looks could kill, Braden would be long gone. Grace jumps up as if she's ready to claw Monica's eyes out, and that's when I notice it. The new purple bruise on her left forearm. When she sees me look at it, she quickly moves her arm behind her back. As Monica grabs my arm and hauls me toward the concession stand, Grandma's advice floods my thoughts and I mouth the words to Grace, "I'm sorry."

Monica and I share a slice of pizza and a Sprite. Phinney bumps up against me and mutters, "That's almost like sharing saliva, Zach-man."

We go back into the gym, where I try to forget about Braden and Grace because the electric slide has started. Monica screams, "I love this dance!" and bounces up and down with her skirt flapping.

Thank goodness we learned this in Puddles' class. The steps come back to me pretty quickly. Backward, forward, turn. I laugh when I see Phinney turn in the wrong direction and try to quickly correct himself.

Maggie is beside him and that makes me smile. Fun is finally starting to register.

Monica and I exchange a look, and laugh. There is never a dull moment with her, and I never have to worry about what to say because she talks all the time.

The next dance is a slow one. Monica's thrilled but this is the moment I've dreaded. I've never touched a girl real close before except in dance class, and that was because Puddles told us it was part of the state standards. I seriously need more deodorant.

I recognize the song from one of the *Twilight* movies.

Every girl in the place screams and gasps like they're going to hyperventilate. Most go running off the gym floor and sit down to watch the "slow dance" couples. This is all new and strange to me but kind of exciting, like I'm a mini-celebrity.

Monica takes control. She turns to face me, grabs my left hand in her right one and puts her left arm up on my right shoulder. She's done this before. The only place for my right arm is around her waist.

Then a miracle happens. Monica stops talking. A slow-dance song shuts her up. I'll have to remember that.

The words of the song are pretty sappy.

I have died every day waiting for you
Darling don't be afraid, I have loved you
For a thousand years
I'll love you for a thousand more

The smell of Monica's hair distracts me from the words. It smells like strawberries. She moves in closer and lays her head on my shoulder. It feels new and awkward and nice. I try to stay off her feet. And then for some reason, Bart flies into my brain.

I haven't thought of him all night, but suddenly I'm picturing him coming back early. What if he comes crashing in here and flips out when he sees me slow dancing to a song that talks about loving his girlfriend for a thousand years? I haven't seen those *Twilight* movies, but I've heard enough to know that there's this vampire dude who does *not* like the werewolf guy making moves on his girl.

Suddenly I get this eerie feeling that I'm the werewolf and Bart's the vampire waiting to rip my neck to shreds. A chill goes down my spine, and I nervously eye the double doors.

No Bart in sight. Just Braden. Beside him is Grace,

looking like she's taken her archery stance and ready to shoot. Which one is she trying to take out? Monica, or me?

I watch, knowing that in the dark, she can't see that I'm looking at her.

Heart beats fast
Colors and promises
How to be brave?

Suddenly the music skips, and the D.J. apologizes for the technical problem and lets the song start over. Then, something surreal happens. Braden awkwardly puts his arms around Grace, and they start dancing. Slow, not really moving much. He's actually touching somebody. A girl. *My* Girl Scout!

I step back from Monica and tell her I need a drink. I have to talk to Grace right now and get Braden away from her.

I feel Sam stepping in front of me. "Don't. She doesn't want to talk to you."

Go home!

I walk to the door, but only Braden is there. "Where did Grace go?"

"I want to dance," Braden says.

"Did Grace leave?"

"Who is Grace?"

"Grace! Grace Elliott. You know, the girl who bought you pizza and soda? You were just dancing with her!"

"Can I dance with you?"

I growl under my breath.

The room starts bouncing when "Y.M.C.A." starts. As long as you can get your body to form those four letters—shoot, even if you can't—everyone is happy. My parents once told me this song has been around since they were kids. I didn't believe them until I Googled it. I hate to admit that a song I like is one my parents used to dance to. There is something wrong with that.

Braden is still begging. "Puhleeeez dance with me! I like this song."

Why not, I think. I grab Braden's arm, laughing. "Let's go, bro!"

Watching Braden on the dance floor is like something I've never felt before about him. He's kind of a goofy dancer, but so am I! He twirls me around, high-fives the girls, and looks pretty darn normal.

The moment ends as someone requests another slow

song, and naturally, Monica drags me away from Braden. As I'm thinking of how to escape and find Grace before she gets away, I notice Braden standing in the middle of the dance floor. His body is rigid, arms straight down at his sides with fists balled, staring straight up at… the strobe light.

Nooooo!

I feel the weight of the earth crushing me.
—Zach

I push Monica so hard she stumbles and slides on her bottom.

Braden!

The earth tilts, and I feel the weight of it crushing me. I manage to race around all the couples on the floor like I'm sashaying down a ski slope, nearly taking some of them out as I cut corners too close.

Panic-stricken, I scream, "Turn 'em off. Turn the strobe lights off!" The music drowns me out.

My legs barely make it to him. By the time they do, Braden has dropped to the floor, and his limbs are shaking. His eyes are rolled back, and the sight of it sucks the life from me. When this happened on LINK day, the teachers and nurse took care of him. But there's just me this time. I take hold of his arms but they feel mechanical, like they're locked. I feel the nausea rising. Something jolts my brain, and I reach into my pocket for the cell phone Mom said I could use in an emergency.

I have to try the password three times before my shaking fingers get it right, then I hit "home" on the favorites menu. It seems like an eternity before Dad answers. I'm sobbing. "Something's wrong with Braden. Another seizure I think. Hurry Dad, please hurry."

By now, the music has stopped, and everyone but the teachers has run for the hills.

Braden grinds his teeth and the sound sickens me. I long for Katy Perry's sweet voice or even Monica's incessant chatter.

The adults surround us, and Mr. Allen, the assistant principal, kneels beside me. "Zach, what do you do when this happens?" he asks.

What do I do? Can't you see? I scream. Part of me dies. That's what I do.

Suddenly Braden stops thrashing and becomes very still, curled in a fetal position.

"Oh, no!" I yell. "I don't think he's breathing."

I bend over Braden, rub his back and rock back and forth. I pray and cry and gasp for my own breath, choking out his name over and over and over.

"No! Help me, Sam! Someone help—please!" Panic is squeezing the life from my lungs.

Someone tries to pull me back, but I continue rocking. Please let Braden be okay.

Where are Mom and Dad, for Pete's sake?

The gym lights slowly start to come up, which gives me a better look at Braden's face. His face and lips look blue. "Don't die on me! Someone help him! Don't do this! Don't leave me, buddy!" I scream, and I lose sight of him through my tears.

Where is Sam? How can he leave me at a time like this?

A blanket appears and is tucked around Braden. Miss Thompson is on her phone asking questions about seizures. I let myself drown in fear for some unending amount of time.

I feel Braden move beneath me. Suddenly I am half laughing and half crying, between hysteria and the horrific reality of it all.

Someone touches me again. I react with a jolt and rear back.

"Zach. It's Dad. We're here."

Finally! I turn and collapse in his arms, practically

knocking him over. I clutch his shirt as I sob, choking and gasping and fighting for sanity.

"He's okay. Braden's coming around." Mom pulls me off Dad so he can tend to Braden.

I gasp as my lungs start functioning again and bawl in my mother's arms like a baby.

• • •

I wake with a mega headache. I had some nightmare but don't even try to remember what it was. The one I will never forget is the one in the gym.

After a long shower, I dress and sit on my bed, staring out the window until I hear Mom.

"I made some blueberry muffins."

I stare at her. How do parents survive this parenting thing? Especially when they have a Braden. How do they just get up after a night like that and make muffins?

"We are having Braden go through some testing. Some people with autism have seizures, and it's not necessarily epilepsy that causes them."

Mom and I are alone at the kitchen table. She is calm, matter-of-fact, and eating a muffin.

"There's medicine to control seizures." She takes another bite.

I eat two. I don't really taste them, but I'm starving. Mom hands me a third.

Maybe there is life after disaster.

"Will we have to pay for the mirrored ball thing?" It's the only thing I can think to say.

"Maybe." Then she giggles and says, "You really hammered it."

I look at her with an embarrassed smile.

Last night, after it was apparent that Braden was going to be okay, I watched the mirrored ball being lowered from the ceiling. I stared at it like it was an evil creature. That ball ruined my otherwise awesome night.

I saw a bin of gym equipment behind me and pulled out a bat. *Perfect*, I remember thinking. I walked to the demonic ball, gave it one solid whack, and returned the bat to the bin. No one said a thing. Mr. Allen helped the custodian clean it up, like it was all in a day's work at Hazard Middle School.

"It's my fault," she says. Her lips start quivering. "He didn't want to go. I made him." And she puts her head in her hands and begins crying pathetically.

It's one thing for me to lose control, but when my mother loses it, it's a new dawning. "Normal" has just moved further on down the road.

36

Zach has a knack for helping others.
But it's OK for him to get help sometimes, too.
–Mr. Berger

I hand Grace a note in math class.

G. Are we still on for archery Sunday? Z.

When the dismissal bell rings at the end of math, Grace turns and glares at me. It looks like her answer is *no*.

• • •

After dinner, I try reading more of *Mockingbird*, but I keep nodding off. The cover is coated with Braden's stickers, as he got the idea to "decorate" it one day. Whatever. Nicotine Nancy is really into this book, and it's actually decent, but it's hard to read much when I'm so tired. My body feels like I'm dragging an extra 100 pounds around. Mom notices when she stops in my room.

"Zach, you have dark circles under your eyes and you

aren't eating much lately. Are you feeling okay?"

Like a truck ran over me. A truck named Braden.

"I'm fine, Mom."

"Let's take your temperature."

She comes back with the ear thermometer and my sisters. "Hmm… well that's normal."

"Maybe he's lovesick," Eva suggests in a serious voice.

Sisters.

Mom smiles. "And Dr. Berger, how did you come up with that diagnosis?"

"He hasn't had Grace over lately, and he misses her."

Mom chuckles. "You should invite her over again, Zach. I liked her."

When I don't answer, she says, "I'm making an appointment for you to see Dr. Peterson. You never know what might be going around."

Like a brother who nearly dies in your arms. Is there medicine for that?

• • •

The phone rings while I am doing my math homework. Dad picks it up downstairs. I can hear his voice moving from the kitchen to the office and imagine him trying to stretch the cord far enough so he can sit down at the desk. *Honestly, just buy a cordless phone!*

I plug my music in my ears so I don't hear the conversation.

Dad calls up the stairway a couple minutes later. "Zach, come down right away please."

I hear him but don't respond. He probably wants me to do something with Braden or collect trash.

"ZACH!"

"Yeah. Fine. I'll be down when I get this math done." I glance out the window. Some snow flurries but nothing serious. No chance of having a snow day off of school at this rate. And I could really use a day to sleep in.

When I go downstairs, Dad is in Mom's office drawing some cartoons—his favorite pastime.

He stands when I come in and looks upset, so I'm figuring I'm in trouble. "Son, have a seat."

Son? He never calls me that.

"I just took a call from Grandpa."

Inwardly I sigh with relief.

"Zachary."

He never calls me that either, unless I'm in trouble.

I look across at him. He's stalling. "Zachary."

Okay, that's twice. Something's up.

"It's Grandma. She had a massive stroke this morning."

My heart starts racing. "What's that mean?"

"It means that blood flow to the brain gets cut off and there is swelling of the brain."

I jump up. "Well, let's go see her! Is she in the hospital?"

"No, Zach. I'm sorry. She's... gone."

"No, I just saw her yesterday. We played chess. She..." I feel lightheaded, so I sit again and lean forward to support my head.

I feel my father's body wrap around mine to hold me. But I just want to be alone with this. I break away and run to my room. I rock back and forth on my bed in misery, gasping loud breathy cries until my body is stripped of energy.

• • •

"Here." Braden has dropped a piece of wadded-up paper on my chest. I knock it to the floor. I can't deal with his little games today. Grandma is dead.

Braden puts his hand to my forehead the way Mom does to check our temperature. "You look sicker than a dog."

I turn my eyes to Braden and nearly laugh. Braden

just used an idiom. You look sicker than a dog. Almost a joke. Not that he was trying to make one.

Braden leaves the room and I sit up on my bed. I kick the crumpled piece of paper back and forth between my feet and finally pick it up. I flatten it out and see a miracle.

Sunday 1:00. GS

• • •

I have only been to one funeral: when Dad's cousin died. I was only six or so and didn't really know June Collins—that was her name. I didn't know her smile or what her voice sounded like. If she had hobbies or favorite food, I didn't know what they were.

And when you're six, maybe you don't think as much about what it means when people die, so it didn't bother me. There were a lot of people crying though, and it made me wonder why Mom and Dad would haul their little kids to such a sad affair when they wouldn't even let us watch movies where animals died.

Grandma's funeral is different. This was someone I loved, and I'm not six anymore. I knew where she kept her secret candy stash. She could anticipate my moves in checkers. In fact she just beat me last weekend when we played.

After the service we are ushered into a dining area to eat. As I take my last bite, I notice someone sitting alone across the room. It is a girl, and she is facing the wall so I can only see her back. But it's enough.

Why is she here? Is she playing Girl Scout here too and volunteering at funerals?

My attention is pulled back when I hear Mom crying. Grandpa reaches for Mom's hand and strokes it. Then he turns to me.

"Zachary. Grandma told me that you talked to her about your brothers."

I freeze.

"She said your imaginary brother gives you advice about Braden."

OHMYGOD. I don't dare look at my parents.

Instead I turn my eyes to where Grace had been sitting. The chair is empty.

I dread the ride home. My parents already have one son who isn't... quite right.

Mom doesn't ask any questions. Not directly, anyway.

"Grandma was lucky to have you in her life, Zach. She loved it when you came over and helped her with her chores and played games… and talked. You have a knack for helping others. That's a gift."

The back of my shirt is soaked.

"But it's okay for you to get help sometimes too."

She thinks I'm crazy. I just stare out the car window.

I repeat things over and over. Questions, things
I've seen, stuff that other people say.
—Braden

From a block away I see her red jacket. Grace is already at the water tower even though I am five minutes early. The butterflies are back. As curious as I am about a girl who can shoot an arrow so perfectly, I am even more curious about how she can forgive a jerk like me.

I have a couple of apples and a package of store-bought cookies to help make peace.

"Hi," she calls out.

She's talking at least.

"Hey. Where's your bike?"

"We sold it before we moved here. It wouldn't work for me in the snow anyway. I don't know how you ride in it."

I hop off and walk along beside her. "I guess we all have our strengths."

She grins. "Maybe I shouldn't teach you my archery

tricks so I can be better than you at one thing."

Whew, she hasn't lost her sense of humor.

"Are we going to your house to shoot arrows?" I don't see any houses in the direction we are walking.

"No, just an old barn where I practice."

"You have a barn?"

"It belongs to a guy my dad works for."

"I have to call my mom and let her know where we are. You know how mothers are. They want to know where you are at all times in case of some national emergency, like telling you when it's dinner time."

Grace frowns. "Don't give your mom such a hard time."

Okay. I was just making a little joke.

We walk to the edge of town.

"How's Braden doing since the school dance?"

I don't really want to talk about him. "He's seeing a doctor to see what's up."

"And you?"

After a long pause, I say, "I'm fine." *We're the "fine" family, after all.*

She stops walking and looks at me.

"That's why I shoot. To forget about stuff." And she

starts walking again.

We reach the barn. She was right about it being old. The wooden siding probably used to be red but is now peeling and weathered gray. One window is missing glass so a board is nailed over it.

Grace heaves the sliding door open. The overhead track groans. When we get inside she switches on the lights and forces the door shut again. She has done this a time or two.

I lean my bike against the wall.

"Cool!"

She grins and nods in agreement.

It is a neat old place with pigeons sitting up on the rafters cooing. Some bales of straw are stacked up against the opposite end wall. I take a deep breath. The sweet smell settles into me.

In front of the bales is an archery target on a stand. A ray of dusty sunlight streams in through the windows. It's like a magazine picture.

Grace disappears into a tiny space, complete with cobwebs, and comes out with a bow and a bag of arrows.

"I'm going to show you what you were doing wrong in Presell's class." I see her teasing smirk.

"Doing wrong?" I exaggerate my shock.

"Yeah. You grip the bow so darn tight with your left hand," she says. "When you release the arrow, the muscles in that hand relax and move, and it throws off the direction of the arrow."

"The same with your left shoulder, neck, and back. You gotta keep them more relaxed, or the power released in those muscles can cause your arrow to go off target."

After a few tries, I improve.

"Bullseye!" I shout when I finally get my first one.

"All right! Now you need to take me to the movies!" Her eyes are shining. I guess she's done being mad.

"And buy you popcorn too, right?"

"With extra butter!" Her voice is smiling as big as her mouth, and my body relaxes.

After twenty minutes and a few more perfect shots, I take a breather. "Your turn. Show me how the experts do it."

"The experts don't use that kind of bow."

Of course not.

"And by the way, you got five bullseyes. You now owe me five movie nights."

"Oh really? Well I better get a job first to pay for all

these movies I'm taking you to."

Grace walks into the dusty closet and comes out with a strange black piece of equipment in her hand.

"*This* is my hunting bow," she says proudly.

She hunts?

"It's a compound bow that has decent speed and accuracy for a kid's bow."

"*That* is a kid's bow?" I can't hide my amazement.

"Want to try it?" She hands it to me, and I barely know where to grab it.

"Whoa! It's heavy."

"Not really, just a few pounds."

"So call me weak!"

She giggles.

"Where did you get this thing?" I stare at its parts and can't believe Grace is into this.

"Dad gave it to me last year for Christmas."

"Why?"

"So I could hunt with him."

"Hunt?"

"Sure. It's fun!"

"What do you hunt for?"

"Bears."

"*What?*"

She bends over laughing.

"Very funny. No really, who uses this bow?"

"Oh, I wasn't kidding about that. It's mine, and I do hunt, but not bears." She giggles again. "I hunt squirrels and rabbit mostly. Sometimes Dad takes me deer hunting."

Deer? I know better than to ask her why a girl would do that. I don't want to get beat up. "Do you eat them?"

"Uh huh."

Of course she wouldn't hunt just for fun. I sit down on a bale of straw, and she sits on another one a few feet away. "Show me." I hand the bow to her.

"It's too powerful to shoot in here."

There's an awkward silence and I look at Grace. It's time.

"Hey." I inhale and let it out slowly. "Can I ask you something?"

She gives me a worried glance. "You want to know where I live."

I look across the distance between us and can't really read her. I go slowly.

"No, it's about something else."

She looks relieved. "What?"

"What were you doing at the funeral?"

And why do you always have bruises and scratches on you?

Why do you take all that cafeteria food and store it like a pack rat in your locker?

And yes, now that you bring it up, where do *you live?*

Her head turns quickly toward me, and she wrinkles her forehead. "Huh?"

"I saw you eating at the church—after the funeral."

Her face flushes pink and she bites her lower lip.

"Whose funeral?"

She didn't know whose funeral she was at?

"My grandma's. Remember? She died."

"When was it? The funeral, I mean."

She's gotta be kidding. I can't help but laugh even though none of this is funny.

"Yesterday. You were there so you should know!" I don't mean to sound accusing but, come on…

"I-I didn't see you." She looks like a cornered mouse.

"Why were you there?"

"I-uh-I was… eating." She sounds defensive.

Duh.

"Were you volunteering or something?"

I sound like my mother. Cross-examining her. She gets up from the bale of straw and picks up a couple of arrows.

"No. Not exactly." She is making this up as she goes.

So what exactly were you doing there? Sitting all by yourself. Eating.

"I didn't know that was her funeral." She picks up one more arrow and sits down again, only further away.

The silence is louder than anything I can say.

The sun is hitting her hair just right, making it shine a reddish color. I can't keep my eyes off her. She is so pretty. *And lying.*

"Well it sure wasn't McDonald's. Why were you…" I stop when I see her flinch. "Never mind. Look, maybe I should head ho—"

"I get hungry." She blurts it out. It doesn't sound like the usual calm and confident Grace.

What?

Her eyes are glued to the barn floor.

"I eat at a lot of funerals." Her words come so fast, she practically stumbles over them.

You're joking. That's like… morbid.

"There's nothing to eat on the weekends."

Nothing to eat.

My mind flashes back to Grace eyeing the lasagna and pie at my house. And all those cookies. The locker stash.

It's stone quiet, and her eyes are still locked to the floor.

Finally she takes a quick peek in my direction like she's checking to see if I've flown the coop. She doesn't look at my face, only my feet.

"At school I get free meals." Her voice is an icy whisper.

Her family is poor and she's embarrassed. Trying to hide it.

"Grace, you don't have to tell me this." I find my voice but only because I don't want to hear anymore.

"We don't have a refrigerator."

My temples begin to throb.

"Or stove." Her voice is shaky.

She's kidding.

"Or... house." I barely hear this one.

Stop it. OHMYGOD. She doesn't volunteer at the homeless shelter. She lives there.

The coldness has left her voice, and she's breathing deep, trying not to lose control. *No, don't cry.* I don't know what to do with a crying girl. After what seems like an eternity, I think of something.

"Where do you sleep? Where do your mom and dad and you... live? Everybody's gotta live somewhere?"

That sends her. She leaps to her feet and lunges at me. Her eyes are black and accusing and... wild.

She starts in and her piercing voice pushes me back.

"I'm not everybody, am I?"

She's holding the arrows up over her head with the sharp points toward me.

I shouldn't have come here.

"Not like the rest of your friends and you with your nice houses and perfect little families."

My family is not perfect.

Grace has cranked up her volume to a deafening level. She's still got the hunting bow in her other hand, and she's waving it around in exasperation. I lean back. She's scaring me.

"We don't have beds! And you keep asking me where I live. Well, we don't live *anywhere*." She gulps in air and keeps yelling, like there's no other way to get through to me but to shove it down my throat.

"We just sleep wherever they will let us park our

trailer. And, and…" She's trying to keep the volume up but it's not working. All that's left is a pathetic choking sound that rips me in two.

She stands and heaves both arrows with all her might. I duck and hear them connect with the barn wall. Holding my arms up to defend myself from the arrows and her words, I yell. "Stop it! Stop it, Grace!"

Her shoulders sag and she drops the bow.

Her face is red and twisted in a painful way, and she no longer looks 13. She looks older. Way older. Her eyes are flooded as she haltingly reveals her deepest sorrow. "There is no mother. She's… dead."

I catch her as she collapses forward in an awkward heap on the floor.

There it is, the answer to my questions—most of them, anyway. I wish I hadn't asked.

Eating funeral meals. Hunting. No mother. What a beautiful mess she is. I guess this isn't the proper time to ask about those bruises. Crazy how a minute ago we were having so much fun.

Crazy.

She lies on the floor with her head on my knee until her sobs turn to sniffles, and her breathing is regular.

"I'm fine now."

I will never believe that line for as long as I live.

Grace sits up wiping her nose. Her face is red and puffy and sad. A Girl Scout, out to save the world when it's she who needs saving.

We both stand and she picks up her hunting bow. I collect the arrows, including the ones stuck in the wall, and hand the wimpy bow to her so she can put it away.

If I were an adult I might say, "Shouldn't we talk about this?" But I'm just a kid and don't even know how to handle my own problems. I have more questions for her, but I don't want to hear the answers.

I push my bike outside and Grace closes the door.

"Sorry about all that."

She's apologizing? I should be the one apologizing—for asking too many questions... for the life she has.

"I had no idea. You look just like any other kid."

Only better.

"I am like any other kid."

With no mother, and a dad who—

I hand her the cookies and apples. She tucks them in her backpack, and we walk back toward the water tower together.

"Thanks for the shooting tips." It's lame, but all I can offer.

She tries a smile. "See you in math tomorrow."

"I'll bring you some more cookies."

"I'll bring you a dead rabbit."

This makes us both laugh a little before we head in different directions. A minute down the road, I stop and look back. The trailer court is not that way. She's headed toward the landfill. What hasn't she told me?

Mom and Dad let Braden get away with murder.
—Zach

Christmas break is finally here, and I can't wait to sleep in. I don't know if it's too much basketball or what, but I am really dragging. I leave my overhead fan on so it covers up family "noise." Unfortunately the fan doesn't prevent morning visitors.

At 7 am Braden crashes into my room.

"Where are my stickers? Did you take them? Where are they?"

I don't answer so he shakes my shoulder and keeps at it. "What did you do with them?"

Now I'm ticked. I throw my elbow into him. "Ouch! You hurt me."

"Braden, I didn't take anything. Go ask Carly and Eva," I mumble.

"NO! I want my stickers." He starts rummaging through my desk drawers and makes a mess, leaving them hanging open.

I roll over and he's in my face. "Give them back!"

"Get out!" I demand with as much energy as I can muster this early.

"I want them back!" he shouts and kicks my bed.

Really? This is the way my break's gonna be? I cover my head with my pillow.

I hear Braden open my closet door and rifle through my stuff. "Can I have these?"

I don't answer.

He leaves and I find out later that he took my shoebox of baseball cards and mixed them in with his sticker collection.

I blow a gasket. "Dad, he's taking my stuff!"

Since the college kids have all gone home for the holidays, Dad is actually home for a few days. "He said he asked."

"Well I certainly didn't tell him *yes*. He can't come into my room anymore. Dad, you need to tell him!"

"Do you really care about those baseball cards anymore, Zach?"

I cannot believe what I'm hearing.

In an accusing tone I say, "Dad you're letting Braden

get away with murder here. Today he's stealing my baseball cards. Tomorrow he'll be taking stickers from some store. I don't think the police will ask the store owners, 'Do you really care about those stickers Braden stole?'"

I turn to storm off, but not before saying, "And I better have every one of my cards back in my closet by noon. In order. By team."

Dad's eyes grow as big as saucers. I can't believe what I just said to him, but I can't help feeling that it's about time. Sam gives me the thumbs-up as I head back to my room.

Maybe I shouldn't have talked to Dad that way, but my cards are back in my closet on time and in order before noon.

"Zach, I'm sorry for saying that about your cards. I have a ton of junk I save, that I haven't looked at in twenty years, but I can't seem to give up," Dad says quietly.

"Oh yeah, like what?"

"Oh, where do I start? My erector set I got when I was eight and all my college textbooks that are molding in the basement."

"And all your broken remote planes. Maybe we're related to the hoarders."

Dad laughs and comes over and gives me his wrestling hug.

"I'm sorry Braden is the way he is. I wish…"

My eyes instantly fill up. *Me too, Dad. You have no idea how much I wish…*

"It's Christmas." His voice sounds fragile. "Let's have a peaceful one."

What's the chance of that?

• • •

WHAM! WHAM! WHAM!

Holy smokes. What in the world? It's been less than 24 hours since the last forced entry, and here we go again.

I was sleeping hard. Not even one nightmare. I hear Braden's voice and the doorknob to my bedroom being worked over.

"LET ME IN!"

WHAM! WHAM! He's pounding my bedroom door. Killing it really.

"Braden. Stop it. You can't come in," I mumble into my pillow.

"Y-y-you can't lock doors. It's the law. You're in trouble, Zachary!"

Me? Right.

I have to explain. It's against the law to lock bedroom doors in our house. Something about safety and gaining access in a fire or another emergency... like when someone wants to steal your baseball cards. I locked my door last night before bed and now this.

BOOM!

I bolt up in bed. Braden has kicked clean through my door. His bare foot is inside my room, sticking out through the gaping hole. Splintered wood is scattered on the carpet.

This is a nightmare. A morning nightmare. Mom is going to freak out.

I hurry to the door in a flash and already hear Braden howling. I attempt to push his foot back through the hole but slivers poke his foot and he howls louder.

I unlock my door and pull it open, which is a mistake. The inward motion of the door pulls Braden off balance from the foot he is standing on, and he falls to the floor. He tries pulling his foot out, which causes the splinters to poke further into it.

Braden screams bloody murder. And speaking of blood, there is some of that too.

Mom comes bounding up the steps two at a time,

followed by Dad, my sisters, and both dogs. My parents gasp when they see Braden and glare at me like I did it. Beulah starts licking Braden's face even though he is howling and flailing his arms around like a madman defending himself from killer bees. I feel like we are in some kind of freak show at the county fair.

Suddenly Carly starts giggling even though she's hugging the bawling Braden. And what Carly does, Eva does. And when Mom and Dad both start laughing hysterically, I wonder if we've all gone crazy. I have to sit down, I'm laughing so hard. The twins roll on the hallway floor until Carly declares she's wet her pants and that sends us all roaring again, except Braden who is still lying on his back wailing with his bloody foot stuck through the door.

Once we all get that out, we help Braden get his foot out of the door. I'd like to think he's learned his lesson, but I doubt it.

• • •

We go to Grandpa's for Christmas Eve dinner. Grandma's empty chair stares at me, and the meatballs taste funny. Then we head to church. Our family has had a rough history of church-going. There was a long stretch when Braden couldn't sit still. One time, when Dad got mad and threatened to duct-tape him to the pew, Braden stood up and yelled, "I hate my Dad!" right in the middle of Pastor Tim's sermon on honoring your father and mother.

The last time I was in a church was for Grandma's funeral. This makes me think of Grace and where she is tonight. I look around half expecting to see her. But then again, there's no food being served, unless you count the stale communion wafers.

The candlelight service is always a tense ordeal as Braden insists on having his own candle. He never pays attention, so last year he dripped wax all over the carpet. Tonight it is Grandpa's pants that get it. Grandpa just smiles and shrugs. I guess when you're that old you don't have a mother who gets all worked up about wax on your Sunday pants. Still, I am relieved when "Silent Night" is over, and we blow out the candles. We've made it another year without burning down Hazard Methodist Church.

Snow is lightly falling as we exit the church. I feel like I'm inside one of Grandma's snow globes. The church bells are chiming "O Holy Night"and I'm hoping Grace isn't alone with her Dad on Christmas Eve.

• • •

Christmas Day at our house is all about eating too much and, of course, presents.

"C-c-come upstairs and see what I made you." Braden's hands are flapping when he says this so I can tell he's excited. He has patched the hole in my door with a sign that reads,

Zach's Room. No Trespassing.

I try a fist bump with Braden but he misses, so I slap him on the shoulder instead. I get a sense of Sam nearby and shiver.

At about 2 p.m. Mom and I deliver Christmas cookies to a nursing home. "Mom, can we drop by where Grace's Dad works with some cookies?"

I feel her look at me but I stare straight ahead.

"Sounds like a wonderful idea Zach, but why can't we drop them at her house?"

Because I still don't know where she lives. "I think she's volunteering today."

Mom is a saint for not asking anything else and for not saying another word about my "other" brother.

The day after Christmas I have a basketball

tournament in Overland, which is an hour away. Carly and Dad have bad colds, and Braden doesn't want to go, so Mom and Eva are the only family in the stands. I keep messing up. Bad passes, missed shots. I only score four points and feel like I'm hauling a train around the court.

"Berger. Get the lead out!" Coach keeps yelling.

Eva comes over and hangs on me after we win 47-38. Mom takes one look at me and asks, "Are you feeling alright?"

"Mmm. Fine."

World's biggest lie.

She feels my forehead. "You're warm."

"Mom, I'm playing basketball. You get warm." I realize I've said this a little too sharply.

We have lunch and nearly a two-hour break before the next game. I lay down on the locker room floor to rest.

"Berger. Get up!" It sounds like the voice is coming through a long tunnel. Someone is shaking me to pieces, and my throat burns.

When I open my eyes, the whole team stares down at me. Coach helps me sit up. My head is throbbing, and I swear I've been thrown in a sauna.

"It doesn't look like Zach's going to be playing the

next game," Coach says.

What?

"Tim, go and tell his mom to meet him at the main entrance in five minutes. Jordan, you help him get his stuff together."

He turns to me with a sympathetic smile. "Zach, it looks like you're coming down with something, and it's best you don't expose the whole team to it."

There's no cure for Braden-itis.
–Zach

"What is mononucleosis?"

"Mono is a virus that is spread through tears and saliva. You probably got it by sharing someone else's drink or fork," explains Dr. Hillman.

I have a sudden flashback to the winter dance—to Monica and me sharing a slice of pizza and a Sprite and Phinney saying, "That's almost like sharing saliva, Zach-man." I groan.

"Also, stress can play a part," Dr. Hillman continues. "When someone's immune system is weak it's easier to get sick. This explains why you've been feeling so tired the last few weeks, Zach."

"Will he need medicine?" Mom asks.

There's no cure for Braden-itis, Mom.

"No, just a lot of rest. He's lucky to be on winter break so he won't miss school. If he feels better he can go back after break's over."

"What about basketball?"

Please don't say I need to miss basketball!

"I checked your spleen and it isn't enlarged. If it were, you'd be out for four weeks. I suggest you don't play for ten days, then come back and see me to be sure everything's okay."

I nod with relief. Ten days will be January fifth. We don't have any games until the eighth.

I sleep most of my vacation. No bad dreams, and very little Braden.

On New Year's Eve, my parents have some friends over. Mom comes to say goodnight and to bring me a letter. There is no return address but I recognize the writing.

Dear Zach (aka Fred),

How is your Christmas break? Dad brought the cookies home Sunday and they were yummy! I liked the gingerbread ones with the white frosting and red-hot candies for buttons. Thank you for bringing them. Did you decorate them?
Mom and I used to do that with my sister.

Sister? This girl is full of surprises.

My dad and I went to Chicago to see her over Christmas. She's nine and lives with my aunt. She wants me to live with her but Dad wants me with him.

I go to the shelter soon to help out. My dad doesn't want me to go but they give me a meal.

No funerals lately, apparently.

I made this for you. The wood is a knothole that fell out of a board in the old barn.

Happy New Year
from your Girl Scout

P.S.: Please don't tell anyone I live in a trailer because the county might make me go to a foster home if they find out.

MY Girl Scout? Wow!
Maybe it's the mono on top of the holidays making me feel mushy, but my eyes get a little wet.

I look in the envelope and shake her gift onto my bed. The wooden knot has a little hole with a piece of twine through it making it into a necklace. I study the wooden knot and rub it between my fingers slowly. It is so smooth. I run the twine across my palm, remembering how tightly I'd been grasping the twine on the bale I sat on the day she told me that awful stuff.

I stare at her letter. 'Don't tell anyone we live in a trailer because the county might make me go to a foster home.' Why would the county care if she lives in a trailer or not?

I look at Braden's sign covering up the hole in my door. Maybe having Braden as a brother isn't as bad as living without your sister and not having a mom.

• • •

The first two days after break I only attend school half days to satisfy Mom. On the first day, study hall with Mad Marlys is a free-for-all.

An announcement comes from Bart, the Self-Anointed Great One. "Berger's got the kissing disease! Girls! Stand back. I know you're dying to kiss him, but you're gonna have to wait a few weeks."

Everyone laughs of course. I just shake my head and pretend to do my art assignment on perspective drawing.

Big-Mouth Bart knows how to get the word out. Someday he'll make it big in the advertising industry.

"I think he got it from me!" yells Allan Ness. The entire study hall erupts.

You're wasting your time in school Allan. Doesn't someone need a comedian?

"Or from me." It's Janet Gallerin and laughter goes off the chart.

Gag. Janet is the queen of Goth from tip to toe. Leather clothes with chains. Three-toned hair and a ghostly skin color. Her eyes have a sort-of vampire look.

Before Mom picks me up at noon, I push a note through the little vent on Grace's locker.

Dear Girl Scout,
Thank you for the letter and wooden necklace.
It's cool. I hung it on the corner post of my bed.
Maybe you could go into business making zillions
more. Your business could be called Girl Scout
Designs or something. Then you'd be rich and
could build a mansion for your family to live in.

I have mono which means I feel like sleeping
all the time.

I don't have a present for you but maybe I
can give you a second dance lesson at no cost.

Happy New Year,
Fred

After school Mom drives me to Dr. Hillman for my ten-day check up. I'm feeling pretty normal, at least on the outside.

"You can resume basketball practice next week, but take it easy. And if you have to kiss a girl, make sure she's a pretty one."

I feel my face flush as he and Mom have a laugh.

I h-h-hate the sound of rain hitting my window.
—Braden

On Wednesday, school is cancelled because we have freezing rain, and the superintendent isn't excited about buses sliding into ditches.

Braden is running around in his Superman slippers turning lights on and off. Eva and Carly are down in the rec room dressing up in old Halloween costumes. Dad went into work early to supervise salting the sidewalks on campus, and Mom is working from home, which means she'll be on the phone all day. I just heard her tell someone it's a great time to sell a house. A half hour ago, I heard her tell someone it's a great time to buy a house. This explains why she's so successful at her job.

I hang out listening to music but even that gets old, so I wander into Braden's room and see that he's on the Internet.

"Spell 'financial'."

"What?" I ask.

"Spell 'financial'." He hands me paper and a pencil.

"Why?"

"I want to look at financial stickers."

"I don't think they make financial stickers." I write the word down anyway.

He Googles "financial stickers" and up pops hundreds of budget-minded stickers.

"See?"

I laugh. "Braden, you're always right."

"I h-h-hate that sound."

"What sound?"

He looks at the window, where the icy pellets are hitting the glass pane. His sensory system is on high alert as usual.

"Braden, we get a day off of school, so you should be loving that sound!"

"I hate that sound," he repeats in a monotone voice as he scrolls through the stickers.

As I leave, I glance out his window. Some nutty kid wearing an oversized coat is shuffling down the sidewalk, trying not to slip.

I watch as the kid continues up the sidewalk holding his hood in place so it won't blow off. He steps off the curb in the direction of the Salzmanns'. Who would be walking to their creepy place on such a bad day? Or ever?

Suddenly the person's legs go out from underneath him, and he falls hard on his back. His head snaps back and hits the curb. Ouch!

I hurry downstairs and dig around in the hallway closet for my binoculars. I haven't used them since Old Man Salzmann's visit. I move to the window and notice the person is up but limping. Although I have the binocs trained on the kid, his hood hides his face. The barking dogs bring the old man out. As the kid steps onto the porch, he turns his head and takes his hand off his hood to point at the howling beasts. The strong wind blows his hood off. I adjust the manual focus on my binoculars and gasp.

No way!

She quickly pulls her hood back up and turns to enter the house with Mr. Salzmann.

No, don't go inside.

I slowly lower my binocs and stare at the house. *Why*

would Grace be going there? Did she walk all the way from her trailer in this bad weather? Should I tell Mom or go over there myself?

My mind is racing. I picture the bruises on Grace's arms and wonder if she's been to the Salzmanns' before. *She wouldn't go somewhere unless she knew it was safe, would she?* I would never go over there, and I'm their neighbor!

I run to the freezer and grab a handful of the leftover Christmas cookies and stick them in a plastic container. I dig through the wrapping paper shelf and find a bow and tape it to the top of the container. Grabbing my jacket, I bolt out the door and wipe out on the first icy step. Ahh! My elbow hits the concrete, but I manage to hold onto the cookies. I continue the treacherous journey across the icy yard and nearly fall again. How in the world did Grace make it all the way from her trailer on this stuff?

This is the first time I've had an up close and personal look at the Salzmanns' mutts. Since they didn't take a bite out of Grace, maybe I'll survive. Naturally, they start barking as soon as they see me. The front door opens. No need for a doorbell, I guess, when you've got attack dogs.

It's Randall, the one who Dad says just got out of

the Army. It looks like he just rolled out of bed. He is unshaven, wearing sweats and his GO ARMY t-shirt. He stares at me like I've just crossed the enemy line.

"Uh, my Mom wanted me to give you these Christmas cookies." Christmas was two weeks ago. "Oh, and maybe you can share them with your guest."

Silence. I move the cookies toward him. After what seems like an eternity, he reaches out and takes them. Without taking an eye off me, he opens the lid, picks one cookie out and dramatically bites off Rudolph's red nose.

I take a quick glance past Randall into the house, which surprisingly looks normal. It has a big bright entrance and a dog lying on the wood floor.

"Thank your mother."

I nod and he closes the door, but not before I hear Grace coughing her head off somewhere inside.

• • •

It's after midnight. I'm exhausted and yet I can't sleep. I turn my lamp on and pull down Robert Frost's poem.

Nothing gold can stay.

I think about all the Ponyboys and Graces and Bradens of the world. I picture their problems and sadness stacked on top of each other and feel hopelessness crawling in. And a need to take control and fix all this madness. Someone has to.

I drift in and out. I sit up on the edge of my bed. The house is so quiet at night.

I pick up my pillow and move to the hall. The nightlight casts a spooky shadow of me against the wall.

I stare at my shadow for a while wondering what I am doing here.

I turn and move toward Braden's room, the land of autism. Standing over him with my pillow hanging in one fist at my side, I take time to study his face. The nightlight allows me to see the rise and fall of his chest. He looks so normal when he's sleeping.

My toes run into a line of soldiers, and they fall like dominoes. Braden doesn't stir. He's got his earplugs in.

Wouldn't it be nice if Mom and Dad didn't have to worry about him and his future? I dreamily imagine Braden as a regular older brother, who doesn't flap or bust through my door. And no one is teasing him or crushing him with a bus.

I drift back to when we were little. We would hide under Braden's covers every time Dad came home from work. I long for that world, the one I can only get to by crawling back into time and into bed with him.

I hear us giggling, knowing that Dad will do the same thing he always does. He'll call out, "Braden! Zachary! Where are you? Where are those little Berger brothers?" And when Dad eventually finds us, he'll tickle us until we can hardly breathe.

Sadly, I can't go back to that time. I fidget with my pillow.

"What are you doing, Zachy?" My body jumps as if I've been prodded with a hot iron. It's Eva.

"Nothing." I whisper. "Going to the bathroom." She is standing in the hallway clutching her thread-worn blanket. In the dim light I see her stare at my pillow.

I toss it into my room and walk to the bathroom, not bothering to turn on the light. My skin feels icy cold yet I'm sweating like a pig.

I return to bed and somehow sleep finds me, but only after the mother of all nightmares.

• • •

Morning comes. My head feels the size of Texas. I'm woozy like I've been on a boat for a month, and my mouth is sandpaper dry. The mono must be back. I try to stand but my legs are wobbly. I sit back down. Eva comes to my door. She spies my pillow on the floor.

Ahhhhh! A speeding bullet hits my chest. I remember it all.

"BRAAADEN!" I scream his name like the devil himself is after me. I half run and half crawl down the hallway to his room, hysterically crying his name, tripping on the hallway runner.

"I'm sorry. Oh God no."

My bloodcurdling screams bring the entire family to Braden's room. His body is gone. They've taken him already. I am on my knees, hands clasped together, shaking my head back and forth. I turn and my parents are staring at me as if they're looking at a madman. Is that hatred or panic in their eyes? I can't tell anymore. I can't tell anything.

I grab at my father's leg but miss.

"Zach, what on earth?" He's got his arms around the twins, holding them back from me.

"I need to make my bed," someone says.

My body stiffens. My mouth halts its moaning. I twist around and stare at what has just walked into the room.

A ghost?

"You're still here?" I manage to squeak.

Braden stares at me and repeats his demand. "I need to make my bed. And fix my army guys."

Dad picks me up from the floor and sits me on Braden's bed. Mom feels my forehead.

"Zach, what's the matter? Were you having a nightmare or something?"

"I need to make my bed." Braden repeats. I have never heard sweeter words in my life. For once, I can't wait to hear him say it again. I reach out and touch Braden to be sure he's really there. He pulls away.

Mom looks concerned. "You don't look well, honey."

You wouldn't feel well either if you thought you just suffocated your brother.

I seem to have no filters anymore.
—Zach

"That was nice of you to bring cookies to the Salzmanns."

The sound of her voice makes me jump, and I hit my right elbow on the sharp edge of my locker door. My other elbow is still tender from the fall on the icy steps. Now I have a matching set. Grace sounds hoarse like she has a sore throat. I'm so glad to see her in one piece that I almost forget that I'm mad at her. She's coughing. A nasty cough.

Ignoring the pain shooting through my arm, I waste no time trying to get some answers to what has been eating me the last few days.

"What on earth were you doing there?" My voice sounds harsh. I seem to have no filters anymore when dealing with this craziness. I've been on edge ever since the whole pillow nightmare thing.

She backs up. "I'm not sure why it is any of your

business." Her voice matches my tone, and she narrows her eyes.

I notice a bandage on her forehead, and she's coughing her lungs up, but I refuse to get distracted.

"Look, I'll tell you why it's my business. Those neighbors of ours are scary, like horror picture show scary. And why in the world were you out slip-sliding around in an ice storm and smacking your head on the curb?"

"You were spying on me?" She spits out her words.

Sick of this, I yell, "No! I don't even know where you live because you won't tell me, so how can I spy on you? I just happened to be looking out my window and saw someone *dumb* enough to be out ice skating on the curb."

Kids have stopped to stare at us. We move over to the side of the hallway.

"Then how did you know it was me?" She hisses.

"I saw your…" My voice trails off.

"You *were* spying." She has that winning look on her face. Are girls always this exasperating?

"I saw your face when your hood blew off. Where did you get that get-up anyway?" I sound mean.

"If you must know, the jacket belongs to someone at

the homeless shelter. They let me borrow it."

"You didn't answer my other question. Why were you at the Salzmanns'? And what in the world happened to your hair?" I suddenly notice it has been chopped off in an uneven way.

She purses her lips and stares at me. No answer.

"Fine." I raise both arms in defeat, slam my locker door shut, and head to lunch.

She calls after me. "I'm just staying with them a while. Zach, it's no big deal."

Staying *with them? No big deal!*

I halt. Turning and walking back to her, I move in so close I can feel her breath on me and see the fiery flecks of green raging in her brown eyes.

I quietly spit my answer in her face. "Yes, Grace. This is kind of a big deal. And here's why. Those Salzmanns are all men. Big men. You're a girl. They're not the type who sit around the campfire singing 'Kumbaya.' They have guns and monster mutts. And you're *living* with them?"

She stands her ground with her chin up in the air. "And just why do you care?" Each word jabs me a little more than is comfortable.

My eyes bulge wide, and through clenched teeth I

bark out, "I *don't* care."

Regretting that comment immediately, I grab her wrists. She flinches and moans in pain. I roughly push up the long baggy sleeves that are covering her hands. "You already have Daddy or Old Man Salzmann or someone grabbing at you and hurting you."

I look down to expose her bruised forearms, but instead I see that one arm and hand is all bandaged up, and the other arm has a nasty burn mark that has blistered.

What the...?

Grace tries pulling her arms away, but I'm so shocked and angry I hang on and keep rolling.

"Who is doing this to you? And why are you looking for more trouble?"

Her eyes swell with tears as she struggles to break my grip. I let go, and Grace stumbles backward, nearly falling. She turns and runs into the girl's bathroom coughing herself to pieces.

I sense that Sam is near and that even he is shook up. The group of students that stopped to stare slowly moves on. I'm too upset to care what they think. When I glance across the hall, I see Miss Thompson in her doorway and can only imagine what she's thinking.

I drag myself to the school nurse and tell her I'm sick. Mom comes to pick me up, and I sleep all day.

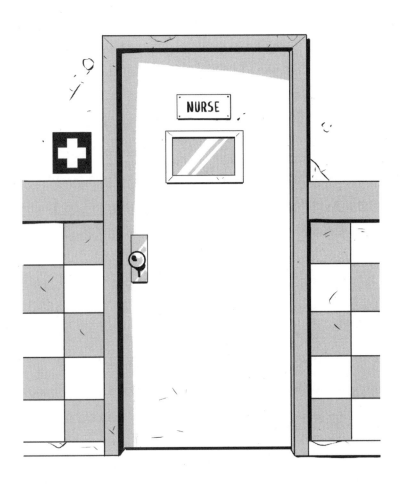

42

I still think Zach is kind of cute,
even if his brother is a little strange...
—Monica

Grace hasn't been in school for three days. To get my mind off her, I thumb through my poetry journal while Nicotine Nancy makes an announcement. "The *Hazard Herald* is holding a poetry contest. I sent in a poem from each student journal. The winning poem will be printed in the paper."

I hope they pick one of Monica's poems. I could use a laugh. Monica is nice to look at, but her writing stinks. During share time we exchange journals and read each other's poems. Monica's are always about the mall and reality shows or winning the lottery. Here's one she handed out to the whole class:

Mirror Mirror in the Mall
Who's the fairest of them all?

Is it the suede Gucci bag
With the thousand dollar tag?
Or the leopard Jimmy Choo shoes
That will match my new hairdo?
ATM ATM in the Bank
Who is the richest one I should thank?
Is it my mommy with her rich mommy?
Or is it my daddy with his rich daddy?

I'm saving it for our twenty-five-year class reunion so we have something to laugh about. Of course, by then, she'll be a millionaire clothes designer and married to Bart, who happens to have a very rich daddy. Ever since the school dance, Monica has been back with Bart. I guess I was just a stand-in after all.

I start thinking about Grace and where she'll be in twenty-five years. Shoot, I don't even know where she is now.

• • •

"Where are you going?" Mom asks when I tell her I'm going for a little ride after lunch.

"Just over to Phinney's to see if he can help me with my bio lab report."

Dad thinks it's great that I bike all winter long but Mom isn't keen on it.

"Honey, I'll drive you. You're just getting over mono."

"Nah, I like riding."

"Well, take the phone with you then. And don't forget your helmet."

I leave Sam at home. I need to do this alone. Plus I realize I am thinking more and more about this need for a pretend brother, and it's not right.

I ride east to the water tower and head down a side path toward the landfill. The ruts and snow make the going rough so I get off my bike, put it under a bush, and walk the direction I saw Grace head the day we left the old barn.

I pass the junkyard and smell the landfill before I see it. Even though it's winter, the stench makes me gag, so I try to breathe through my mouth. Perched on top of a little hill, I look out onto the mounds of trash. I check the other direction to see if I can see any trailers. Nada.

To the left of the landfill is a small woodsy area. The trees barely camouflage a junky horse trailer covered with a tarp.

I don't know why Grace was headed here, but there's

no sign of a mobile home. As far as I know, the trailer homes are all in Northwood Court on the other end of town.

As I make my way back to my bike, I hear a clanking sound and voices. I look back and notice two people beside the horse trailer. I move in closer. It's Grace and her dad. I duck down and peer through the bushes. I can't hear what they are saying, but her Dad's voice is rough and loud. Grace disappears into the trailer. Her Dad walks toward the street.

Grace said they lived "wherever they will let us park our trailer." I thought she meant a house trailer. People don't live in horse trailers.

I hop on my bike and ride to Phinney's.

"Maybe it's a lifestyle choice to live there, Zach-man."

Grace told me not to tell anyone, but Phinney is my best friend.

"Some people don't want the government in their lives so they go live in the mountains. Grace's dad apparently chose the landfill."

"Phinney, you can't tell anyone. I don't want Grace to get in trouble."

"Whatever you say my friend."

I wonder who the real Grace is.
—Zach

Last night I wrote a note to Grace and dropped it in front of her as I entered math class.

Dear Grace,

Sorry about the blowup. I was just so shocked to see you at the Salzmanns'. I can't believe you're staying there. Are you related to them or something? I can't sleep because I worry about them hurting you. They look like crazy people.

When Braden does something weird I don't want people asking me about it. I feel like it's none of their business. But I guess they're trying to help. I have someone who is trying to help me with Braden. Sometime maybe I'll tell you about him. Do you have someone helping you?

Zach

P.S.: What happened to your face and arms and hair? My grandma always said tea with honey helps a cough.

Phinney gave me a folded note in social studies.

So you do care.
Meet me at the old barn at 10:00 Saturday. GS

I have a bad feeling about this, but I bike to meet her on Saturday anyway. I stop at the water tower wondering if I should turn around. I take in a big breath and continue to the barn. The door is slightly open, and I see Grace doing some target practice. I want to confront her about the trailer she lives in, but she'll accuse me of spying again.

"Hi." My voice is flat. Grace turns when she hears me at the barn door but doesn't say a thing. If she's not talking, I may as well leave now.

Suddenly I wonder who the real Grace is. Are her stories about her family all made up, like my Sam? I already have Braden to worry about. And myself. The last thing I need is someone else to lose sleep over.

But Grace is right. I do care. I like being around her. She is different, smart, and full of surprises. But maybe she is as messed up as me.

Grace comes over to pull the door back enough to get my bike inside. I stand with my hands in my coat pockets. I want to look at her. I always want to look at her. But I avoid eye contact. All I can think of is our last conversation by my locker and me seeing her injured arms and accusing her of things that she probably had no control over.

"I'm not related to the Salzmanns."

I steal a look at her and wonder how such a pretty girl can come from such an ugly situation. She's wearing a knitted hat over her chopped hair.

She continues. "They take in homeless people."

What? And do what with them? She registers my disbelief.

She nods. "Yeah. They're so nice."

That wouldn't be the word I'd use to describe them. But I'm keeping my mouth shut.

"My dad and I are homeless. Well, we had the trailer but that wasn't much of a home."

Got that right.

"I saw it." My confession comes out easily.

"You saw what?"

I swallow hard but hold her stare. "When I saw all those bandages on you at school and then you weren't in school for a while…"

She leans her head back and looks ready to bust.

She won't like this part.

"I saw you walking toward the landfill after the first time we met here so I…"

"Spied."

Biting my lip, I try to nod but my head doesn't move. I am caught in her deadly stare.

"Well, it was just a place to sleep really." She looks away and continues as if my discovery doesn't really matter. She had come here with things to say.

"And Dad—he works most of the time and I'm in school or volunteering so we weren't really in the trailer much anyway." She sits down using a bale as a backrest.

Her words spill out. "But now that it's been so cold, we had to use more than one space heater. And that's what caused it."

Caused what? I feel like I've caught the beginning and end of some mystery movie but dozed off in the middle somehow.

"The day we didn't have school because of the ice

storm? Dad wouldn't let me stay in the trailer. He said I'd freeze to death. The libraries and churches were all closed. It wasn't my day to volunteer at the shelter so I had nowhere to go, and they don't like me hanging around at his work."

I finally find my voice. "Why can't you guys just stay at the homeless shelter? Isn't that what it's for?"

"Dad doesn't want anyone to know about our situation. In fact you're the only one who knows, and I haven't told him you know."

And I don't want to know any of it.

"He won't accept any help. And mostly he's afraid that we'll be separated, that I'll have to go to a foster home if the schools and social workers get involved. That would kill him."

"So he thinks our scary neighbors are better than the shelter? Does he have a clue what kind of people they—" My voice is growing louder.

She cuts me off. "I heard about them at the shelter, and Dad checked them out. They help all kinds of people. Disabled people, war vets who can't find jobs or need an arm or a leg. People just down on their luck."

An arm or a leg? What is she talking about?

"Mr. Salzmann's wife and daughter were killed last year by a drunk driver. He got a bunch of money from a lawsuit plus insurance money and is making a memorial in his backyard in honor of his daughter."

Which explains the late-night chainsaw noise.

"He used some of the money for his own rehab, but the rest he is using to help people who need a break. And Randall is using some of the money to research ways to disarm IEDs."

"IEDs?"

"Improvised explosive devices. Randall was in the Army in Afghanistan. His job was to disable roadside bombs. One exploded and ripped off his leg. He's had over twenty surgeries, and now he's working on ways they can use robots to disarm the bombs instead of people."

In that old camper on the street. How can I live right beside them and not know any of this?

"He and his buddy, who lost both legs, just landed a grant to work on this."

"But I thought you said your dad won't accept a handout."

"He cut a deal with Mr. Salzmann and is fixing a vehicle for him."

"So you're gonna live there now?" I still am not buying this.

"Well, that wasn't the plan," she replies. "The day after the ice storm I walked back to the trailer so I could change clothes and go to school. Dad was at work." Her words are fading away.

I look out of the corner of my eye at her. Her hand is still bandaged.

Don't tell me anything more. Please, no more.

"It was so cold." Her voice is a whisper. "Our gas space heaters had been off for a while since no one was there, so I turned them both on. But it wasn't enough. So I turned on the gas hot plate too." The color has drained from her face.

Stop! I shake my head back and forth and feel tears stinging my eyes.

"It was my fault." I have to lean in to hear her.

"Somehow my sleeves caught fire when I reached across to turn it down. When I tried getting the sweater off, my hair caught on fire."

No. That beautiful hair.

"I rolled in the snow to get it out. I walked to the station, and my dad borrowed his friend's car and brought me to the emergency room." She is out of steam.

I can't speak. I glance at her forehead.

Reading my mind, she reaches up and touches the bandage. "I hit my head on the metal doorframe when I was trying to get out of the trailer in a hurry. Just a few stitches."

I walk over and sit down beside Grace. I put my hand on her bandaged one, and she leans her head on my shoulder. After a minute, I finally get the courage to ask her the dreaded question.

"Those bruises on your arms. Grace, is someone—hurting you?"

"No. No. That was the crazy guy at the shelter. I wasn't the only one. He would grab people and not let them go. He wasn't trying to hurt us, but he is so big and strong. He's not there anymore."

"And the cuts and scratches on your wrists and hands? You're not trying to hurt yourself?"

She looks shocked at my suspicions. "I would never do that. No, those were from digging through bushes and wire fences to try to find the rabbits I had shot with my bow. And one time my knife slipped when I was skinning a rabbit, and I accidentally cut myself." She points to her scar.

She can tell I'm having a hard time absorbing all this.

"We would make stew with the rabbits. You know—to eat."

She holds my gaze, and I have no choice but to believe her. "So you wear long baggy sleeves to cover them up." It wasn't a question.

She exhales loudly and smiles. That million-dollar smile. "And now I'm your neighbor."

After a long silence, I find my voice. "You did a lousy job cutting your hair." She smiles and lets out a big sigh.

It's not very warm in a tent.
–Grace

Well, if Grace was my neighbor, she's not anymore. I go to the Salzmanns' to see her after basketball practice. I figure if Grace isn't afraid of them, why should I be? Peter comes to the door. "Moved out yesterday. For privacy I can't discuss guests." He says it like he's a hotel manager.

> Grace,
> Why are you homeless? I mean what happened so you guys have to live in a trailer?
>
> If you don't want to tell me, it's okay. And where are you now? Peter told me you left.
>
> Zach

I wrote that note two days ago, but Grace hasn't been in school. I rode my bike to their trailer twice, but no one was there, so I stuck the note through her locker vent.

Today she comes to school with icicles hanging from her hair. *What now?* I stare at her. I'm tired of asking questions.

"It's not very warm in a tent."

She's upgraded to a tent. Nice.

During math I stare at the back of her head. The icicles are gone but her uneven haircut reminds me of the fire, and by lunchtime I can't stand it. "I need to talk to you."

We sit together at lunch for the first time, but neither of us eats the burgers on our tray. "How come your dad doesn't have a house for you guys to live in?"

"My mom died of cancer. My parents thought they had adequate insurance, but not for cancer I guess."

"So your dad spent all his money on your mom." That didn't come out right.

"Dad sold our house, cars, furniture, everything to pay her medical bills. And then he lost his job. He just wanted to be with her those last few weeks. But it turned into six months, and Dad's boss couldn't keep paying someone who wasn't in the courtroom everyday."

The courtroom?

"My dad is a lawyer." She answers my questions now before I ask them.

"Couldn't you guys stay with relatives?"

"We did. With Aunt Belle. But after Mom died and the economy tanked, his cousin gave him a job fixing cars. Avery stayed with Aunt Belle, and I moved here with Dad."

I'm glad you did.

"Peter Salzmann said you moved out."

Tears come to her eyes. "We're at the homeless shelter."

We throw away our cold food.

• • •

I write a note to Grace during science and stuff it in her locker.

Grace,
I am sorry about your mom. That really sucks.
I don't know what I'd do if one of my parents died.
I bet your mom was amazing and that you are
like her.

Zach

I have friends. They are things, not people.
—Braden

It's game day. We play our archrival, Allentown, and the team is pumped! If we win, Bart is having a party Saturday night. I have a great feeling about this game because my mono is pretty much over, and my energy is back.

"Come on Braden. We'll be late for school." I realize I'm wasting my breath. There is really no hurrying Braden.

"NO!" Braden shouts at me. "I-I-I-I'm not late for school. I can never be late for school. Miss Cynthia will be mad at me."

Sam's patience is growing thin. I hear him drumming his fingers on the counter. But I refuse to let Braden or Sam ruin this big day for me.

I take a deep breath and let it out slowly. My patience at 7:45 am isn't the best.

"Let's leave him," Sam suggests.

I head toward the door. Braden still has on his

Superman slippers. I make one last effort. "Get your shoes on, and then we can walk to school and count all the cool cars driving by."

Braden looks at his feet, pondering my idea. His face moves to his 'all right then' look. "Let's walk to school and count cars." He states it like it was his idea and repeats it five more times.

Sam groans. I've given up trying to get Sam out of my brain.

Braden puts his shoes on in his usual slow-mo. I feel like my clothes are going out of style waiting for him.

"Let's go, Zachary!" he says, like he's been waiting for me. "Y-y-y-you're going to be late."

I can't help but smile. I smack him on the back and laugh. Sam scowls.

"Goodbye boys!" shouts Mom. "Good luck at your game, Zach. We'll all be there to cheer you on."

We count 58 cars on the way to school.

As I walk into school, I calculate the number of hours until game time. Nine hours.

It's hard to be in a bad mood on game day, but it's kind of a downer that Phinney is mad at me. His girlfriend, Maggie, is a cheerleader, and since my lunch friends thrive on humiliating cheerleaders just because they're cheerleaders... it doesn't sit well with Phinney.

"Zach, my man, you're either with Bart and his mob or not."

I dig around in my locker for what I need for my morning classes and head to homeroom.

Braden and Miss Cynthia wander past with his backpack sagging down his back. I bet his keys and who knows what other useless junk is in it. Braden doesn't have a locker to store things in because he can't figure out how to work the combination lock. For one whole week he had a key padlock but he claims he lost the key. It's probably stashed with his collection.

Sam reads my mind. "You can't keep walking him to school and expect to be popular." I nod. I'll have to figure out how Braden can get to school without me second semester. I continue to bring the point up to Mom and Dad. "Braden should be with his own friends and not me all the time."

"In an ideal world, that would be great. But right now, you both go to the same school, and your father and I need to get the girls to school and ourselves to work on time. It's your job to do this for us."

It's my job?

"Which reminds me. You have to babysit for the girls and Braden the night of my big Starlight Gala. This year we are expecting to raise enough money to build another home for a low-income family. Dad and I are counting on you." She smiles that mom smile that leaves you with no suitable comeback.

Yeah, and just who can I count on? I'm a kid, not a parent. I need friends, not a ball and chain ruining my chances for a normal life. And Dad, why aren't you ever on my side?

The announcements come on. Principal McMillan goes through the usual items: lunch menu, after-school activities—including our game with Allentown—and a reward for anyone who knows the responsible party who plugged the boys' toilet again.

Mr. McMillan drones on. "One last announcement today. The winner of the seventh-grade *Hazard Herald* poetry contest is—Zach Berger! Congratulations, Zach! Look for Zach's poem in the Herald!"

Cool! I wonder which poem Nicotine Nancy submitted for the competition?

The day goes fast. A math quiz on ratios is a cinch for

me. Pizza pockets with mystery meat inside for lunch. We have a fun badminton tournament in gym where I kill everyone, even last year's reigning champion, with my quick wrist action. When science ends, Miss Thompson wishes me good luck as I head out the door.

"What are you? The teacher's pet?" It's Bart's voice. "She didn't wish me good luck."

"Maybe it's because I need luck and you don't Bart."

"Ahh… yes. I have talent on my side."

And modesty.

As I hurry to the locker room after school, I round the corner by the cafeteria and collide with another student. In an effort to keep upright, I grab her shoulders and hold on. "Whoa! I'm sorr—"

"Zach, it's you!" And I hear Grace's laugh. She smiles up at me.

It takes me a few seconds to realize I still have my arms around her. Embarrassed but also feeling a warmth move through me, I drop my arms and move back.

"Hi. Hey, I'm sorry. I don't want to be late."

Grace laughs again. "Okay, I hope you win your game. See you tomorrow."

Awkward.

Running backwards, I say, "Yep! Wish you could make the game." *And that you had a mom and a house and someone to give you a better haircut.*

The Allentown Tigers come out of the girls' locker room with bright orange jerseys that look like they just came from the factory. A roaring tiger outlined in black is on the front of them.

We are the Hazard Hornets, and although our uniforms aren't new, they do look sharp with a big gold hornet on black.

"Go eleven!" I can hear Dad yell during warm-ups. Braden follows. "Go eleven. C'mon, Zachary. Go eleven. Go eleven. Go eleven."

Coach Piper meets with us in the locker room before the game starts and announces the lineup. "Justin Overby and Bart Hurtle as forwards, Jordan Green and Zach Berger as guards, and Too Tall Tim Lyons as center."

All right! I've never started. I keep my eyes trained on the coach to avoid Adam Johnson's eyes. He usually starts.

We run out and sit on the bench as the starters are announced. The cheerleaders are doing their thing, and I see my family. Phinney is in the student section. I'm not sure if he's here to watch me or to see Maggie cheer. I can't let him distract me now.

For the first half of the game we are in control with a six- to seven-point lead. I hold my own and am in and out of the game, sharing time with Adam. I make one jump shot from my sweet spot to the left of the free throw line and just miss a three-pointer that rims out.

Too Tall Tim does a great job rebounding and follows up on shots missed. Bart has been called for traveling twice and is getting frustrated, so Coach pulls him. At half time, Coach tells us we need to be getting more shots off.

"You can't score if you don't shoot!"

When the second half starts, the Tigers gain momentum, and the score is soon tied at twenty-nine. The coaches of both teams spend the third quarter off the bench, yelling at us to do this, do that.

Allentown has a player they call Bear; I guess it's because of his woolly hair. He is their sharpshooter and pours it on in the fourth quarter. Pumping in three shots in a row, he puts Allentown ahead, 44-40.

I feel a sure thing slipping away. Bart is wearing down; he's been playing most of the game. Justin, our other forward, has put in 10 points, but now he reaches in and thumps Bear on the arm. The ref blasts his whistle for Justin's fourth foul. Coach pulls Justin and subs in Adam for me, and I move to Justin's forward position. I've only played this position in practice a few times.

Bear is at the free throw line for Allentown, bounces twice and gracefully arcs the ball into the hoop. All net.

We battle back and forth and I'm struggling to defend Bear. I haven't made any points since subbing for Bart, even though I've taken three or four shots. The Tigers widen their lead on us, and with just three minutes remaining in the game we are down by eight.

Bart returns and I get a breather. Adam sinks a three-pointer. The seconds tick away and I'm back in. Too Tall, Bart, and I shoot our hearts out. But our opponents do the same. Jordan fouls a player the Tigers call Glue—probably because he can't jump—to stop the clock with nine seconds left.

Coach calls "time" and tells us his plan. Bart and I will stand near the centerline during the free throw. Too Tall will get the rebound (assuming Glue misses the shot, which is doubtful) and throw it to Jordan, who will catapult it to either Bart or me for a breakaway layup to win the game.

Glue makes the first free throw. Now we're down by two. The second one goes up and spins the rim and whips out to Too Tall.

Seven seconds left. The small crowd is on its feet screaming.

Too Tall whips it to Jordan so hard that Jordan misses it, and it rolls over the centerline and into the waiting hands of Allentown's Bear. He dribbles with a look of joy on his face, celebrating with five seconds to go. I charge toward him with all that I have and steal it mid-dribble before he knows it's gone.

Turning, I pump the ball to Bart who takes two dribbles into a perfect layup, tying the game. The ref's whistle screeches. Bart's been fouled and the shot counts! No time remains on the clock, but Bart gets to take the free throw. When the ball goes through the hoop, the fan noise is the most exciting I've ever heard.

I wish I had a brother.
—Phinney

This morning when I pick up the *Hazard Herald,* I flip to the sports page. Only high school sports are covered, so there's nothing about our great win over Allentown. But it doesn't matter because I already got the best comment after the game from Phinney. "That steal was something out of the NBA highlights, Zach!"

As I fold the paper, I notice my school picture on the lower right corner of the front page.

Poetry Winner Chosen By *Herald.* When you live in a small town, I guess this is news. I turn the page to see my poem. *No! Not this one.*

I never put a title on it. I barely remember writing it. It was after the school dance when I was pretty wigged out about Braden and Grace and all the kids in the world with no say over the insanity in their lives. Nicotine Nancy had given us an assignment to write about bad vs. evil, so I did. My parents are going to take me to the nearest asylum if they see this.

World, you wear such a lovely disguise.
Your sunrise golden greets me every morning
What amazing blues are your skies.
But just what evil are you hiding?

Life, you trick me with your beauty.
You hand out babies for all to kiss
And plenty of puppies warm and cuddly.
Do you think I am blind to this?

In your backroom you are hiding it.
Another dark and evil future
Deciding who will be your next culprit.
Gambling over us like a gangster.

You are mining for my soul
But you're not going to get it from me.
Why are you looking for total control?
In the end it will be me who will be free.

Ugly things can rise from your beautiful places.
The mirror of life cannot lie

Look around at all the frightened faces.

I have only one question. Why?

I put the paper in the recycling bin and force my thoughts to Bart's party. A stupid poem is not going to ruin this day.

I have never been invited to a girl-boy party. Curiosity about which girls were invited is getting the best of me.

I haven't told Mom and Dad about the party. I'm not sure they would be okay with the girl-boy part. If I said I was invited to Bart's party and didn't mention girls, I wouldn't be lying exactly.

Around 4 pm, Mom floats into my bedroom humming "Sweet Caroline" and twirling. She holds two dresses against her body and extends her right arm as if she's dancing with a partner.

She sings a couple lines. Neil Diamond. Why do they make songs where you can actually understand each word?

"Which dress should I wear to the gala?"

I point to the pinkish dress with white flowers all over it. It looks more like a gala dress than the black one—the one she wore to Grandma's funeral.

"You're right. It's more perky."

Mom's sounding happy. Now might be a splendid time to tell her about the party. "Mom, you deserve a new dress! Why don't you go out and buy a new one?" I try to not sound like I'm up to something.

She laughs. "Zach, I'd love to! But I don't have time to go shopping before the big event tonight."

Wait! Her gala is tonight?

There are too many rules and words.
–Braden

"You haven't forgotten about babysitting, have you?" she asks as my stomach drops.

"No, no. I'll be here."

It's useless to even mention the party. I'm stuck here. Mom co-chairs this enormous fundraiser, Stargaze or Starlight whatever, every year. How did I forget?

"The girls checked out two movies from the library today. They can watch one and then need to be in bed by 9:00. Braden should like the movies they picked out."

And what about me? Will the movie be better than Bart's party? Will watching my sisters and brother win me some points with my friends?

In the middle of my pity party, Sam whispers, "I have a plan." And he drags me off to my room.

"AHH! OUCH!"

Something's wrong with Dad. Mom tears downstairs with me behind her.

Dad is in the living room with a fishhook stuck to the seat of his pants and the twins giggling. Mom works to help free him. I guess the hook is left over from Braden's bike repair/tool box project. I smile. For once I'm not the victim of Braden's antics!

By 7 pm, Mom and Dad are ready to leave for the gala and announce they'll be back at midnight.

"Say, Zach?" It's Mom, and I know that tone of voice. She's going to ask me to do just one more favor. Like, will I sign in blood that I'll take care of Braden for the rest of my life?

"Don't forget to sort the laundry and empty the dishwasher tonight. And have you picked up your room this week? It looks like a tornado went through."

Bart's party starts at 8:00. I call and tell him I'll be late.

"It's stylish to be late. The girls will notice when you walk in later than everyone else." Sam can be very convincing.

Carly and Eva sit on the couch to watch a documentary about some goofy scientist who discovered animals once thought to be extinct. Braden is in the room but isn't watching the movie. He is laying a bunch of keys out on the carpet end to end.

"Make us some popcorn." Carly is being bossy.

Listening to Carly's whining and watching Braden with his stupid keys, I can't help but boil over at having to babysit when I should be on my way to Bart's.

"Braden, pick up those keys, or I'll chuck them all out the window," I order.

"You c-c-c-can't."

"Oh yeah, watch me." I pick up a handful of keys, go to the front door, and throw them in the snow.

By the look on Braden's face, I realize this was a mistake. He looks terrified. "My keys! My keys! They are my favorite ones."

"You've got a couple hundred other keys, Braden, and they're all alike."

"Get them!"

"No way."

He runs upstairs and locks the door to his room. Why did I do that? I don't need to invent more problems, so I go out and dig around in the snow. This is nuts. I don't know if I have them all, but I bring the wet keys in and push them under Braden's door.

"Th-Th-Thank you, Zachary." I hear sniffling.

"You don't get him, do you?" I feel a lecture coming on from Sam. I am letting him into my head way too much lately. "Autistic people like their things. Their order. Their routine. Let me deal with him for once."

What are you, the autism whisperer now?

I sit down and wait for the girls' movie to end. "Time for bed!" I announce when it's over. Eva wants to know why I changed into my church shirt and why I smell funny. Why do sisters never seem to notice anything until you don't want them to?

"You didn't make us popcorn."

"Carly, it's too late."

"Read us a book."

So I do, and by 9 pm they are sound asleep. I go through Braden's schedule with him. "Stay upstairs and count whatever you want, and then go to bed when the timer goes off. Don't answer the phone, don't call anyone, and don't answer the door." Not that anyone would come at this time of night anyway.

"Make me popcorn, Zachary."

"Make your own."

Maybe it will work. Go to the party, leave early, get

back before my parents do.

I let both dogs out to pee and grab Mom's cell from the counter. Maybe I can call Grace if the party is boring. Her dad bought her a phone after the trailer fire.

As I close the garage door, I notice Mr. Salzmann standing by his fence staring at me. "Where are you going this time of night?" His voice sounds eerily accusing.

"Just out for a short ride." I don't care what Grace says, I still think he's scary.

"Where are your sisters?"

Creepy question. "At a sleepover." I wasn't about to say they're home alone with Braden.

I spend the ten-minute bike ride calculating what time I'll have to leave the party in order to be safely back before Mom and Dad return. 10:30 should work.

It is January, and no one in their right mind rides their bike at night in Indiana. Thankfully the temp is above freezing, but the wind bites as I ride.

I am nervous, not only about leaving the house but about this party. I don't know what happens at a boy-girl party, but it's guaranteed to be better than that school dance. No spinning balls, no Braden.

Bart told us to use the back entrance to the lower level

of his house. Loud music leads me to the door from a half block away. Phinney and Cockroach are the first ones I see. Maggie is holding Phinney's hand. Phinney would never be invited to Bart's party except Maggie is one of Amalia's friends and Amalia is Monica's best friend and of course Monica is there.

Phinney looks at me but says nothing. If he's here at Bart's party then he's bought into the Bart popularity club just like I have so he has no reason to be mad at me anymore.

I see Bart across the room dancing with Hannah Holliday, or Hungry Hannah as most of us call her. She's always eating and always hunting for a boyfriend. Bart waves and announces my entrance. "Zachary Berger is in the house, ladies and gentlemen!"

Does he do that to draw attention to me or to himself?

I wave, feeling a little embarrassed. I guess it is fashionable to be late.

Phinney loosens himself from Maggie and strolls over. "Glad you could make it, Zach-man!" Apparently he's decided to renew our best friend contract after all.

I bet Sam is giving me a disgusted look.

Phinney drags me to the other side of the room

where six or seven guys are sprawled on an old green sofa. They're all reminiscing about the glorious win and sipping on sodas.

A handful of girls are standing around the sofa, pretending to listen but mostly giggling and whispering among themselves. Monica asks if I want something to drink, so I join her at the folding table that holds the popcorn, a tray of brownies, and two coolers of soda.

"Great party, huh?" Monica comments.

"Sure is!" Why do I always talk too fast and too loud to her?

"What took you so long to get here?" she asks.

My parents don't know I'm here, and I'm supposed to be babysitting. And I have to get back before they return, or I'm a dead man.

"Uh, well, I was doing some weight lifting and had to shower before heading over."

I've never weight lifted anything at home except grocery bags.

"Let's dance," Monica says.

"Um," I glance around, looking for Bart.

"He's over there," she says, pointing to Bart. "We broke up."

Really! Is that because he forget to mention one day that the heavens revolve around you?

"Bummer."

"Not really. Let's go!" She pulls me toward the dancing couples before I have a chance to think about how Bart will kill me, even if she is his ex.

She laughs and dances like she was born to do this, and I'm having so much fun that I don't care about Bart or what my dancing looks like.

"I'm thirsty!" Monica shouts after a couple of songs. Several girls cling to Monica near the drinks and lean in to whisper. They look at me and giggle. I can feel the heat crawl up my face.

I glance at my watch. I feel Sam giving me the "no sweat; it's still early" look, but I'm thinking I should call Braden. I don't want to wake him though. Maybe I'll leave earlier than I planned.

"Come on!" Monica grabs me and I'm back on the dance floor. I can't believe Bart's parents haven't been down to check on us once, or at least to tell us to turn the music down.

During the next dance break, I pull my cell phone out and see a bunch of missed calls. All from home. So much for telling Braden to not call anyone.

Suddenly I get a terrifying thought. Maybe Mom and Dad got home early, and they have been calling me. Holding my breath, I listen to the first message.

"I'm scared. When are you coming home? I'm s-s-s-scared."

Sure enough, it's Braden. I listen to the second message. "I'm gonna make popcorn now."

My phone vibrates. Another call from home. What if this one is from Mom or Dad? I swallow and walk toward the doorway, wondering what excuse I could possibly come up with that would warrant leaving my babysitting duties.

I coax my voice to sound normal. "Hello."

"Zachary!"

Whew! It's just Braden again. And he's on fire.

It's hard for me to focus. My brain is like a
Best Buy store where all the TVs are on a
different channel and I can't turn any of them off.
—Braden

"Zachary! Fire!" I hear the muffled sound of something falling.

"O-o-on me! I'm on, I'm on fire! Popcorn burned. House b-b-burning." He's screaming, and all the blood in my body has gone to my head. I feel the room sway.

"Get out!" I scream at Braden. Everyone has stopped dancing.

Braden's sobbing. I can hardly understand him. He's breathing heavily.

"Can't get upstairs. The-the smoke…" and I hear him coughing. Smoke. Smoke kills. *My sisters!*

"BRADEN! GET OUT OF THE HOUSE AND TAKE EVA AND CARLY WITH YOU!" My vocal chords have reached their limit.

"My k-keys. My s-s-sticker collection. They… They'll get burned up." His crying is more like a wounded animal howling. Torturing my ears, my soul.

I will my desperation through the phone. "Get OUT, Braden. Get everyone out NOW!" I pound each word. The music has stopped. Unaware of my friends' stares, I start swearing. The party is over.

I drop my phone, turn, and tear open the door. My shirt cuff catches on the storm door handle but the ripping doesn't register. Nor does the bloody gash on my forearm caused by the rusty door edge.

Lifting my bike upright, I race alongside it, place my left foot in the pedal, and leap onto the seat, already in flight mode.

This isn't happening.

What does Braden mean he's on fire? Why is something burning?

I hear Sam in my ear trying to reassure me. "Braden exaggerates. The popcorn probably just got burned in the microwave, and it's a little smoky in the kitchen."

For a second I feel my body relax and realize I always overreact. For a second I notice how cold it is. My coat is back at Bart's house. Something's burning in my left arm.

I should never have told Braden he could make popcorn. I should have done it for him. He always burns it. I'll have some explaining to do to my friends on Monday morning for leaving the party. Maybe I should go back and explain. I slow my bike.

Then I hear something other than my heart pounding in my chest. A police siren followed by the distinct and air-piercing sound of a fire-truck horn. My body stiffens, and my heart wants to leave my chest as I hear the sirens get closer.

Somebody called 911.

I taught Braden how to do it a couple of years ago. Mom was furious at me because he kept "practicing," which meant the police were at our front door several times.

A few blocks to my left, I see numerous vehicles with flashing lights scream down Emerson Street. Our street is off of Emerson.

Oh God, Braden. Carly and Eva. Oh no. No! Horrifying visions of my little sisters trapped in the smoke form in my head. *No. Don't think that way. Tell me this is another nightmare. I'll wake up soon.*

I turn forward again and careen into the curb to

my right. I over correct to avoid jamming into it and lose control. The bike leans and tilts left, putting me at a freakish angle to the ground. As the back tire spins around to the front, the bike separates from me. My left hip hits something rock hard on the street. I don't even wait for the skid to stop. I push myself off the pavement with my left hand and will my feet to spin and follow the sound of metal hitting the street. I hop on and continue my flight down Poe Street.

All of the streets in this area are named after poets. I start thinking about street names and dead poets and Ponyboy and Robert Frost's poem.

My left hip is killing me, but I focus on my destination. *Did Braden call 911?* We used to play cops and robbers in the basement, and I'd make him use the play telephone to call the police. I'd use the toy handcuffs to lock up the robbers, who were either my sisters' dolls or my sisters.

My brain is going haywire. *Focus, Zachary.* I am soaking wet.

I wish I could fly over the treetops and land in my yard and see that everything is fine. Just burned popcorn, nothing more. Braden and my sisters would be sound asleep. False alarm.

I do not see the car parked in front of me until it's too late. I brake and swerve. I manage to avoid the back bumper, but the side mirror meets my right shoulder, and I land with a thud on the street. The street is slippery and wet. The pain in my right shoulder and arm overcomes the left hip pain.

I lift myself off the ground and find my bike. The handlebars are bent and the seat is missing. I straighten the handlebars as best I can.

Maybe this is one of those nightmares where you keep trying to get somewhere, but stuff keeps happening and you can't make it. I'll wake up in my own bed, and I'll remember that I was at the best party a seventh-grader could ever hope for.

Without a seat, I have to stand up and pedal. My legs are on fire. I'm forgetting to breathe. And my shoulder is more numb than painful. Breathe, breathe.

The sirens have stopped, but I can see the rotating flashes of emergency lights in the night sky. Right over where I live. Maybe the fire is at the Salzmanns'. They're always burning tires in the backyard. Or maybe... and I get nauseous thinking of it... maybe Old Man Salzmann set our house on fire to teach me a lesson for spying on him. He saw me leave.

This is taking way too long. Did I make a wrong turn? I've biked these streets hundreds of times. Not at night, but I know this like the back of my hand. No, here is Dickinson Ave. I'm on track. The fenced-in elementary school is straight ahead. I'm okay. I haven't lost my mind. Yet.

My left hand is so slippery on the bike handle. As I pass under a streetlight, I see blood streaming from the forearm gash onto my handgrip. I'm pedaling but nothing is happening. I fall to the right, and in the dim streetlight I see that my chain has fallen off. It has also started to snow.

The bike is toast. I leave it and start to run at full speed. Rather than go way around the school grounds, I climb the fence. I feel like I'm in my own little action movie and am wondering if I'm the hero or the bad guy.

The possibility of this nightmare being real washes over me. I gasp between the sobs coming from me and taste a wet saltiness in my mouth. My tears mix with snowflakes and I can barely see. I can't risk running into anything. *Focus.*

I race across the schoolyard and feel my knees buckle

in the sand of the long-jump pit. I fall, but at least it's a soft landing. I can finally see the fire trucks through the Tessings' backyard.

Oh no! They are *at our house.* I will my legs to move faster and use my arms to pump harder. My chest is burning as I suck in the icy night air. *Breathe, breathe.*

The Tessings' garden fence halts my sprint. Something has punctured my leg. I reach down and pull a wire from my thigh and continue racing around the garden, away from the cliff and toward the edge of my nightmare. *Wake up, please wake up.* I refuse to believe this is real.

I rush around the Tessings' house. No! I see flames coming out the front windows of our house on the first floor, and emergency vehicles fill the street. I rush up to a fireman. My lungs burn, and I try speaking but nothing comes out. The fireman grabs my shoulders and I scream from the pain.

"Andy. I've got a kid here in shock. Take him into the ambulance."

No! I pull away. I will my voice to say something. *Sam I need you please! Where are you?*

"My brother an-and sisters. Get them." I am so dizzy. Don't pass out.

"Which rooms?" he yells. I am staring in disbelief at the hot flames scorching my face.

He gets in front of me, inches from my face, and tries again. "Where do they sleep?"

I stare into his eyes and see a reflection of the flames. Without looking up, I point to the second story, not knowing if there even is a second floor anymore.

My knees sink to the ground, and I want to die. Something warm and wet is running down the inside of my legs.

I see it again. The edge of the cliff.

This Andy guy is on me, dragging me to my feet and trying to lead me toward the ambulance. Adrenaline snaps me back, and I fight his grasp with the last ounce of energy I have. I run to the open door of our house where smoke is spewing. Like a giant claw, two firemen haul me back and sit me down hard on the cold ground. They put something heavy and warm around my body.

Two firemen come out the front door through a billowing cloud of smoke. They are carrying a stretcher. Ice floods my veins. I start to shake. Ambulance Andy steps in front of me to block what a kid should never have to see. But some morbid part of me needs to, so I shift, and through the smoke I see them pulling a sheet over… someone.

Terror fills my lungs, and I hear a sickening moan that I don't even recognize as my own.

No. My body starts heaving.

Andy has set me firmly back down and is squatting in front of me saying something about parents. Everybody seems to be yelling. The noise of the water hoses and the chaos in my brain drown me.

All I can do is shake my head back and forth. *Sam, come and help me.*

Another stretcher and another sheet. *Oh God, no! Please, no.* Unstoppable sickness builds like a tidal wave. I don't want to see who it is. But I need to.

I like the yellow fire trucks.
I don't like red ones. Just yellow ones.
—Braden

I beat on Andy until he loosens his grip on one of my arms, giving me just enough time to lurch forward before he tackles me again. The stretchers are only about twenty feet away. I'm on all fours scrambling to see the faces on the stretchers, but my eyes are stinging from the smoke, and I inhale a cloud of it. Coughing, I pull away from Andy's hold on my ankle and claw forward. It's dark and bright all at the same time. The glaring and swirling lights of the emergency vehicles cast just enough brightness on the scene to show me something I never ever want to see again. There are no faces on the stretcher. The sheets are completely covering the bodies. Dead bodies. My sisters are dead. I left them alone to burn to death.

I feel an ugliness eat at my insides. And yet I can't look away. All I see at the top of both stretchers is red hair tumbling out from the sheet. Carly, Eva. I vomit all over Andy.

I'm in the ambulance, and someone is checking my blood pressure and wiping my face. It feels cool. *What happened? Why am I in an ambulance?*

A man leans over me. His face slowly comes into focus. It is bleeding from scratches. Something smells horrible.

"Hey. I'm Andy, an EMT."

The sound of his name jerks me into remembering where I am and to a sitting position. Carly and Eva.

I vomit again, this time on myself.

"Where's Sam?" *Don't tell me he's been hurt, too.*

"Who?"

"My bro-my brother." I spit pieces of vomit out. "Where is he? Is he okay?"

"Where is your brother's room? And your sisters'?"

Why is he asking about my sisters? They're dead.

Andy has me by the shoulders and shakes me. "Ahh!" My shoulder shoots pain through my neck.

"Hey kid, stick with me. Where are the bedrooms?"

"Upstairs. On that side." I point, but I am so disoriented in the ambulance that I have no idea where the house is.

"There's no one left upstairs. Only the dogs were up

there." Hank and Beulah. "Think, kid. Where else would they be?"

"The dogs?"

"NO! Your family."

"Mom and Dad aren't here." Thinking of them sucks me into a deep dark hole, and I moan and toss my head back and forth. "Don't tell them! Don't tell them!"

Andy drags me out of the ambulance. My hip is killing me. The outside walls of the house are crawling with fire, mostly on the right side. Andy has a tight hold on me to keep me from collapsing. My left arm is wrapped for some reason. The stretchers have been moved. I start to sob uncontrollably.

"Exactly WHO was in this house tonight?" Andy yells to gain my attention.

My throat burns and I choke on the smoke.

"My brother and…" I can't say it.

"Who else?" He was in my face now.

"My sisters." My voice cracks and sounds pathetic.

"Where are your parents?"

At the mention of them I drag my fingernails down my face. They depended on me to take care of my siblings. They'll hate me. *I* hate me. And I start beating my head with my fists.

"Kid! Stop it. Hey, stay with me. What's your name? And where are your parents?"

I won't tell him that.

"His name is Zach Berger. And his parents are at a fundraiser."

The voice is familiar. Mr. Salzmann. The policeman asks him questions while Andy drags me to the other side of the yard.

I can't stand up anymore. I collapse forward in a fetal position, close my eyes, and wail. Braden is still in the burning house. He is burning up just like my sisters, and it's because I'm a selfish fool. I had to go to a party and this is what I get. Throw me in and let me burn too.

I think about Braden and Carly and Eva being trapped and madly looking for me to help them. Was it burned popcorn that started a fire, or wacko Salzmann? He saw me leave. Grace doesn't know how evil he is. I bet he burned her trailer too.

As I rock back and forth, I imagine Braden calling me. "Zachary!" He is pleading. "H-h-help me Zachary!" I cover my ears. I can't stand it.

Someone is rubbing my shoulder. I blink my eyes a

few times and notice Superman slippers beside me. "D-d-did you find the rest, the rest of my keys?"

I don't know if it's the slippers or the keys question that brings me out of my fog and to full attention. "Braden!" I leap up and fall into him with hysterical relief, holding his smudged face in both hands. "You're alive. You're okay."

Andy yanks at Braden and asks him in an accusing voice, "Were you in the house? Where are your sisters?"

"I like the yellow fire trucks. I don't like red ones. Just yellow ones."

"Braden, I'm so sorry. I shouldn't have left you alone. Oh, thank God you're alright."

"D-d-don't cry, Zachary." He pets my head like I'm a dog. "I was, I was hiding in the bathtub in the basement. I-I-I called 911 like you showed me."

Andy summons two firemen, and they grill Braden about Carly and Eva. He just keeps asking them about their yellow fire trucks. I let my head fall against Braden's chest and wail like a baby.

"He's in there." Braden announces this in his flat tone. I stare at him. *What did you say? He who?*

"He's in shock," said Andy. *No, he is autistic.*

"Hank and Beulah are d-d-dead." Braden's second

announcement.

"Ahhhhh…" My moaning voice is raspy and dry. Not the poor dogs, too.

I feel sick and wrong inside and so very, very tired.
–Zach

"The dogs are over there." A fireman motions to the side of the ambulance. My eyes follow where he's pointing. I rush over and pull one sheet off. Hank! I pull the other sheet. Beulah. Dogs, not girls. Red hair, like my sisters.

A sense of relief mixed with grief over our dead pets and the realization that my sisters are still in the house sweeps through me.

The smell of burned dog hair makes me gag.

"Where have you been, kid?" A stern voice of a police officer is grilling Braden, who looks like he just took a shower with his clothes on.

My brain shifts and I stumble to the officer. "This is my brother. He's autistic."

The officer gives me a "so what" look. Another person who doesn't have a clue about autism.

Frantically I turn to Braden, "Where are Carly

and Eva?"

"They're in the b-b-basement. I put them in the tub. With water."

The two firemen fly inside the front door but return in a few seconds. "The upstairs floor has caved in, so the door to the basement can't be reached."

"There's a back entrance to the basement!" I cry.

The officer and the two firemen race to the back of the house. Andy and I are on their heels, dragging Braden with us. They try the door but it's locked. One fireman rams it with his shoulder. Nothing.

"It's got a deadbolt." *No. NO! My sisters are locked in a burning dungeon with no way out.*

The officer barks. "Get the axe!"

"No time. This side of the roof is gonna go any second. Shoot the lock!" the fireman yells.

"NO!" I scream. "My sisters might be on the other side."

My chest feels like someone is crushing it, and I have to squat down and try not to pass out. I'm slipping into that familiar dark place again. I make every attempt to stay with it.

"I-I-I've got the key."

We all look at Braden like he was heaven sent. The lights from the flames and the fire trucks illuminate his face.

Braden pulls out a lanyard with dozens of keys on it. I squeeze my eyes shut in disbelief. It will take forever to try all those keys. Maybe I threw his basement key out in the snow, and it's still there. When I open my eyes, Braden is handing a single key to the fireman like it's no big deal. The fireman rushes to the door and, miraculously, the key unlocks it.

Both firemen disappear inside, and we watch the flames licking the roof with an intensity I've only seen in movies. In a thunderous crash, part of the roof over the basement door caves in. The massive cloud of smoke forces us to move back toward the swing set. A deafening explosion follows and rips the basement door area wide open. Sparks rain down on us and I'm gulping smoke. My eyes are stinging and my muscles are tight. I look around and panic when I realize I haven't heard from Sam for a while.

"He went in." Braden's voice is expressionless as always.

"Noooo!" I dive forward but Andy pulls me back. I feel

a painful loosening where my arms meet my shoulders, and my throat is raw. I give up and sink to the ground.

If anything happens to Sam… and my sisters… I crawl inside myself. The only one I'll have left is Braden. Just my brother and me.

I can't just walk around and live like nothing happened. I need to fix what I messed up. But this can't be fixed. I can't bring dead people back.

Ahhh, Sam. You were the one normal thing I could count on. I can't lose you. I bolt to the front of the house, where I see Mom and Dad standing with the police chief. They look frantic.

I run toward Dad's Honda sitting in the neighbor's driveway. I know the key will be in the ignition. "No one steals a '98 Honda with no air or radio," he always says. I jump in and lock the doors. This is my chance to fix things.

My hands shake. "Turn the key." I hear my voice, but I barely recognize it as my own. I squeeze my eyes shut and turn it. Vroooooom. *Okay. I've got this.*

I can't hear much over the roar of the engine, but someone's pounding on the windows, yelling at me. *They should really step away so they don't get hurt.*

Why can't all these people see I need help? Serious help. Don't let me do this. Somebody please save me from myself.

I close my eyes to picture Dad's hands and feet and concentrate with every cell of my brain to recall the next step. When I open my eyes, I see Dad's face in front of the windshield. "Zachary, get out!"

Reach foot to pedal. I'm too short. I scoot up and push the pedal. A roaring sound, but the car isn't moving. There is so much screaming. My jaw is aching from clenching my teeth.

I try the other pedal—no sound. That must be the brake, so I hold my foot on it.

I picture Dad's hands on the shifter and can see him pulling it down when he backs the car out of the garage. That's what I'll do. I yank it down. Nothing is moving. Then I remember my foot on the brake, so I let it go.

NO! The car crashes forward into some bikes, and I hear screaming. I hit the brake with all the power my leg has. I slam forward and hit my chin on the steering wheel. This is harder than I thought.

"You'll kill somebody!" I hear someone say. *I already have.*

Tears fill my eyes and my nose is dripping. I sniff and

swipe at my face to clear my vision. My aching fingers grip the wheel. How does a car go backwards? I fiddle with the shifter and ease my foot off the brake. I'm barely moving, so I push the gas pedal, and the car flies backward. There is some serious yelling, and I hit something—hard. I crush the brakes and jerk to a stop. My head whiplashes back and then forward into the steering wheel. Where is Mom when I need her?

Someone is smashing the window on the passenger side with something. There is an explosion by my left ear. I've backed into the street. *Now how do I go forward again?*

My ear is burning. I reach up to touch it and find it wet. Bloody.

I push the shifter down and the car lurches ahead. Some nuts are beating on the car.

Steer, turn. Too far. My hands are slippery on the steering wheel. Sweat, or maybe blood. Dad should really be working with me on my driving. I turn the wheel back, now the other way. Finally, I'm weaving my way out of the cul-de-sac. Luckily we live near the edge of town, and soon I'm headed into blackness.

I feel a rush of relief. I made it. It occurs to me that I've been working on an escape plan ever since LINK

Day, when I realized this thing with Braden wasn't working for me.

I hear sirens again. *Now what's burning?* I feel drained and wonder if my escape plan is doomed. I have no money. I can't go back and face my parents and life without little Carly and Eva. Exhaustion causes my arms to drop off the wheel, making the car veer to the left before I grab it again.

I drive down the middle of the road because the ditches are so… close. Even though it feels like I'm flying, the dashboard tells me I'm only going 35 mph.

It's hard to think, and the siren sounds like it's in my backseat. This plan isn't working.

I maneuver the car around a sharp bend, brake haltingly to a stop, and turn off the lights. I don't even notice I've left the engine running. I get out and sit in the ditch and sob.

"I need somebody!" I gasp at the words and shiver. "Sam!" My weak scream goes unanswered. "Who is going to take care of me now?"

The snow has stopped, but it's deep in the spot where I am sitting. My body shivers, and my stomach lurches, mostly from smoke and self-pity. I notice the stars. They look lonely somehow, so far away. Maybe they need me to join them. We could take care of each other.

I feel sick and wrong inside and so very, very tired. I wrap myself into a fetal position.

The police car rams the back of Dad's car. The last thing I remember is seeing it slide toward me in slow motion. I make no attempt to move.

Heaven is a quiet place, maybe a little too bright. Dimmers might help.
—Zach

"Hi, Zach. Hey! He's waking up, finally." Eva's sweet angel voice. She's on my left side, petting my white wrapped arm.

"It's about time!" Carly is on my right, poking my other arm.

I get to be in Heaven with my sisters. Someone has granted me more than I deserve. I attempt to sit up, but everything feels tight and sore. I thought there was no pain in Heaven.

"Zachary, honey, we're here. You're all right. We're all fine." Mom's crying.

Fine? Then why are people crying?

"We're so glad you're okay, Zach." It's Dad's voice and he's crying too. I've never heard Dad cry before.

It takes me all of a split second to realize that this is

not Heaven. I'm in the hospital.

I bolt upright and feel a sharp burning pain shoot up my arm with my sudden movement. I've pulled an IV partly out of my forearm.

I look around. Braden, Carly and Eva, Mom, and Dad. But no Sam.

I jerk my head around in desperation and breathe heavily as if I've just been pulled from a shark tank. I dart my eyes back and forth to take in my surroundings. "Where is he?" I push the sheets back and try to get out of bed.

"Take it easy, Zach." Dad is pushing me back into the pillow.

I attempt to shout but my voice is a weak, pathetic whisper. "Carly and Eva got out?" I begin to cry in disbelief. "But not…" I sob and rock my head in my hands.

Carly and Eva crawl up onto my hospital bed, and I hug them with as much strength as I can. Mom and Dad have the three of us wrapped in their arms. Through my tears I can barely make out Braden, who is standing by the window flapping his bandaged hands. *What has this done to him?*

"Why were you in the basement?" I manage to

squeak out.

"Braden woke us up because he wanted to watch another movie," Carly explained.

"Y-y-you said I c-c-c-could have popcorn." Braden's voice sounds even. "You told me to p-p-put the microwave on the popcorn setting but that's not r-r-right. Don't do that, Zachary. When you make popcorn, don't do that. Don't do that. D-d-don't do that Zachary."

I went to Bart's party and left them alone.

Dad finishes the story. "Braden said the popcorn bag started on fire, so he used an oven mitt to grab it, but that caught on fire too. When he dropped it in the sink, the flames found the curtain. There was a frying pan in the sink that had oil in it, so that probably fueled the fire.

"I tried putting it out with water, but the fire blew up bad!" said Braden.

"That's because water makes an oil fire worse, Braden. You were lucky to only get mild burns on your arms." Mom's voice is quivering.

"We filled the tub with water and sat in it. I saw that on TV once when a house caught on fire." Carly sounds proud of herself.

I look over at Braden and his wrapped arms and

hands. Overcome with the terror Braden had to have felt, tears stream down, and I reach out my good arm to him. Everyone moves to make room for Braden to sit by me. I lean into him and sob uncontrollably for him, for me, for all of us, and repeatedly choke out in my most desperate voice, "I'm sorry, Braden. I'm sorry. It's all my fault. I'm so sorry."

When I've nearly cried myself out, I notice Braden clutching his lanyard with dozens of keys.

He picks out one from the bunch and holds it between two fingers to show me. "I made the fireman give it back to me."

What is Braden talking about?

"If it wasn't for that key, the fire department wouldn't have had a way to get to the girls in time." Dad isn't having much luck trying to get his voice to sound normal either. "When the roof caved in blocking the doors, the firemen took Eva and Carly out the basement window."

I stare at the key. That key saved someone? Was I there? The key blurs and suddenly I'm so tired.

The last thing I remember is Braden's flat voice saying, "Your Sam didn't make it out."

• • •

Phinney comes to see me. "How's it going, Zach-man?" His smile is genuine, and he pats me hard on the head.

"Just another day in paradise."

"Yea? Paradise sounds scary."

I nod. "A lot of things are scary."

Phinney gives me a long, deep stare. "Zach. It takes all kinds, remember?"

I turn toward the window but see nothing but blur from my tears. "I'll make it up to them. When I grow up and have kids, I'll let Mom and Dad and Braden all live with me so I can take care of them. And we'll get new dogs."

After a long silence, Phinney makes a suggestion. "You better buy a big house."

This makes me laugh, which causes me to double up in pain because my ribs are bruised, and my shoulder and hip are scraped up pretty bad. Phinney comes over and hugs my head and then punches my arm, which hurts even more. My outsides pains will heal in time but I wonder about the inside ones.

The guys stop by after school Monday to sign my cast. My arm was broken during the bike ride from Bart's house. So much for basketball.

Jordan checks out my face. "You look like you've been in a fight, dude! Man, what does the other guy look like?"

"Yea, there are easier ways to miss school you know." It's Bart. He's been standing in the corner of my hospital room and hasn't said a word until now.

My face got cut up pretty badly the night of the fire. When the police car slammed into Dad's car after my "driving lesson," it slid into the ditch and miraculously missed me. But the barbed-wire fence I tried to climb over to escape from the police did not.

I don't mention my driving lesson to my friends, but I tell them all about Braden's key saving my sisters. When they leave, Bart hangs around. He talks about basketball and asks about the hospital food. "I better let you get your beauty rest," he finally says. He stands by the door longer than necessary. "Tell Braden I have some keys he can have."

We all make mistakes.
–Miss Thompson

They don't keep people in the hospital very long. A couple of days and they send you home, even when there's no home to go to. My parents rent a small, furnished house near the middle school that belongs to a retired couple who winter in Arizona.

Braden has barely left my side. He says he is "taking care of me."

Today we are playing cards. When I change positions, a pain shoots up my arm.

"Ahhh! My arm's killing me."

"MOM!" Braden yells. "Something's killing Zachary!"

"No Braden. I mean my arm hurts. It's just a saying. No one is killing me."

He goes across the room and sits in the rocking chair and stares at me. I wonder what he's thinking.

Miss Thompson stops in. She talks. I can't. The sound

of her voice chokes me up. She asks questions and tries to convince me we all make mistakes. Finally I manage two whispered words. "He's gone."

She nods and tears fill her eyes. I close mine. It's still so painful.

For months before the fire, I had been meeting with her secretly again so she could help me cope with Braden and get over Sam, but she said it wasn't enough. She wanted me to see a psychiatrist. I said I would but I didn't.

"I'll start seeing someone. With my parents."

When I open my eyes she's gone.

Grace comes by and kneels next to the recliner I'm sitting in. "Zach, I was so afraid when I heard about the fire." She knows about fires.

She grabs my hand and says, "I'm sorry." Her skin feels warm and soothing. I lean my forehead against hers and finally manage a broken whisper. "I'm sorry for you, too."

"For me?" Her words are shaky.

"You lost your mom, your home. You're poor."

She whimpers, and I wipe her tears with my thumb. "I'm not poor. We just don't have much money. I have my dad and sister. And decent hunting skills." She smiles at this. "And you."

I mop my eyes with the back of my hand. My nose is a dripping mess. How does she stay so strong with all the junk that has happened to her?

"There are things you can learn from people who are different than you," she says.

Our eyes lock for a moment before she drops my hand and leaves.

Sometimes the endless years ahead with Braden overwhelm me.
—Zach

I ask Dad to drive me to our burned house. Not much was saved, and Dad's car is toast, but we still have Mom's vintage van to get us around. As I get in, I notice dog hair on the seats and fight back tears.

We sit in the car and stare at the charred walls and what's left of the garage. And cry.

"I messed up, Dad."

He reaches over and takes my hand. "There's plenty of blame to go around, Zach. We put too much on you and weren't paying attention to how it was affecting you."

We sit for a few minutes, remembering. This is the place my parents brought my baby sisters home from the hospital; it's where I scribbled red ink on Mom's new wallpaper. I was three, and as soon as she got done lecturing me, I took crayons and drew some more on it.

My bedroom is gone and everything in my junk drawer. The seashells I collected with Grandma in Florida. My baseball cards.

I would never find out if the Twinkies I stored under my bed really last twenty years. Mrs. Likens, my fifth-grade teacher, said they had enough preservatives to keep them for that long. I used my allowance to buy some to see if she was right. I only had 18 years left before I knew for sure.

My plastic snake collection is gone too. I loved putting them in my sisters' beds and in the bathtub faucet so when Mom turned the water on, she'd scream bloody murder.

"Everything's gone," I whisper.

"We had too much stuff. In fact, I had so much junk in front of that basement window, I'm shocked the firemen even saw the window to get the girls out." His voice cracks.

Dad and I get out of the van and stand where the front door used to be. "How do you think Braden got out?"

"We have no idea. It's like someone carried him right through the walls. It's a miracle."

I think about that for a minute. I push my shoe around in the ashes. I stoop and pick eight keys out of the soot.

"Maybe Braden can start a new collection." I smile at Dad through the blur.

● ● ●

"It's time for your appointment." Mom and Dad drive me once a week to see Dr. Miller, who has a counseling practice a half hour away in Brookton.

At that first session, I admitted how great I thought it would be to have a normal brother and how I pretended I had one. It was weird having my parents hear me talk about Sam.

"Tell me about him," said Dr. Miller.

"At first it was just wishing. Then it became an obsession. Having someone to help me cope became a need. This sounds nuts, but I had entire conversations with him."

"Did it help?" asked Dr. Miller.

"Well, it helped calm me down… at least sometimes. At first Sam helped me see the better side of Braden, but then he was like, 'Braden's a loser. How are you gonna fit in with him around?'"

"And other times, the whole idea of pretending made me sick, like I was slipping away. In fact, that's when the nightmares started, where I was being pushed off a cliff.

I kept hoping someone would help me or help Braden."

"What did your friends think of Braden?"

"I don't know. Some were cool with him. Others… were mean and made fun." I started to cry and it was hard to say the rest. "I didn't want people to connect me with Braden because…" I glanced toward my parents. "Sometimes he's just so… weird."

Mom flinched.

Today we talk more about Braden.

"Braden does stuff that makes me feel so sad, and my parents say he won't ever be able to live on his own. Maybe when I'm older all this won't bother me so much. But right now it does because I'm trying to fit in and be almost 13, and I'm selfish I guess."

Dr. Miller nods.

I wait a long time to say more. "I'm scared." I barely get it out.

My throat is tight. "Scared of what Braden's going to do next. Today, tomorrow, next year. Always waiting for the next time he's going to get hurt or do something embarrassing. And I'm really freaked about what will happen when Mom and Dad aren't around anymore." Whispering is the best I can do.

"You mean who's going to take care of him?"

That is it. Right there. My eyes are flooded, my nose is dripping, and breathing is hard. I hold my head in my hands and nod. "Because... I don't know how to take care of him and be happy at the same time."

After a miserable minute of sobbing, I take a deep breath and straighten up. Mom has a tight hold on the tissue box in her lap. Dad is leaning forward staring at the floor with his hands clasped.

Dr. Miller continues. "That's part of why you're here now. To start talking about all this and make plans. Anything else?"

It takes me a while to get the nerve to admit it, especially in front of my parents. I nod slightly and wipe my face with my sleeve. I'm not sure I can say it. "I have these nightmares. I thought I..." That's when I break down. "I dreamt I hurt Braden."

I hear Mom sucking in air and Dad say something I can't repeat.

"I just always got the feeling no one was doing anything to deal with Braden."

Maybe I shouldn't have said that.

I can't escape it. The fear, and now the guilt. Especially

since the fire. That was my fault. I left them alone and I can't forgive myself.

My poor parents. This is blowing them away. Maybe all this talking will make things worse.

As Dr. Miller begins to speak again, I have trouble focusing on his words; flashes of fire and Sam interrupt.

"Zach, there is a cost to caring. You have reacted to the trauma of having a brother with a disability fairly normally. But you also have symptoms similar to PTSD—post-traumatic stress disorder—and a secondary disorder called compassion fatigue, or sometimes simply called 'burnout.' We can become emotionally drained or think that we have to do something to prevent or stop bad things from happening. A brother like you, who has an enormous capacity for feeling, is sometimes at a higher risk of fear and pain because you care so much. Nightmares and high anxiety, sadness and depression, are not uncommon. Survival and coping strategies vary."

PTSD, survival. Too many words today. The floor in the office has an interesting pattern. I trace it with my eyes.

"For you it was creating an imaginary friend to talk to. Someone you could trust with your feelings. As you said, your 'friend' sometimes helped you see the benefits of having a brother like Braden, and sometimes he was quick to point out the pitfalls. All of it was to create a balance so you could handle reality and not go off the deep end, as we say."

Dr. Miller asks me about Sam. "Do you know who Sam really was?"

I shrug and stare at a photo on his desk. Dr. Miller has his arm around a boy wearing a superhero shirt.

"Sam was you. You basically counseled yourself by giving yourself Sam. He was your own best advice. You listened to both sides of every situation and made your decisions. In fact, people like you put doctors like me out of business!"

Keys. I hear Mom jingling them in her pocket. I think we should go.

Dr. Miller goes on, "We are all vulnerable to the catastrophes that impact our lives. When things happen to the ones we love, we become the victims too because of our connection to them. Zach, your brother—"

"Keys!"

My interruption stops Dr. Miller's runaway comments.

"He had the key!" I shout. Dr. Miller looked puzzled.

"Braden does stuff that makes no sense to me but they work for him. They... those keys, his key collection that I thought was so stupid. He had a key that saved my sisters! That's normal. No. That's rock-star normal. It's like he has a super sense about stuff. A super power."

I stopped to catch my breath. "All this time... I thought Sam was some kind of hero. But, no. It's Braden who deserves to wear the cape! He is my SUPER-Bro."

"Like this guy." I poke at the boy in the photo before walking out the door. "From now on it's just Super-Bro and Me, my new S.A.M."

• • •

I don't care what anyone says about imaginary friends. I needed Sam. Maybe he was the scared part of me that couldn't cope or the brave part that made me accept things. The only thing I'm sad about is that he was never real.

My parents have figured out a schedule where one of them is home now every day after school. We have talks. "We don't expect you to take care of Braden when he's older," said Dad. "There's lots of services to help him find a job and support his independence."

So maybe Braden won't be living with me after all.

Dr. Miller put my parents in touch with a group called Indiana SIBS, an organization that offers camps and stuff for families of kids with disabilities. He told us that life shouldn't revolve around Braden. That's not going to be easy.

Phinney stops by often to play video games and talk. "Bad stuff happens to everyone, Zach-man. Are you gonna blame Braden for junk he can't control the rest of your life or just let him be your brother?"

When I tell Phinney about Sam, he looks at me real hard. "You don't need to imagine someone else to fix your world. You have it right in here." He points to my chest. "And if that doesn't do it, give me a call." Good ol' Phinney. He has often told me he wishes he had a brother. I guess we're all wishing for something we don't have.

I'm trying hard to take Dr. Miller's advice about reality. Every morning when I get up I tell myself that I'll look for positive things going on with me and accept that Braden isn't going to be cured.

The worst part about the fire was that my stickers burned.
—Braden

I am in no mood to celebrate my birthday but "you only become a teenager once," Mom says. Monica calls and tries to convince me I should have my first girl-boy party, but I choose paintball.

"Shooting your friends? You have to be careful with your arm, Zach," Mom says.

"It's just a game Angela, and Zach's cast is hard as a rock." Dad is more excited than me about this. I think it's because when he was young, there was no money for fun stuff like paintball.

I invite Phinney, Bart, Justin, and Too Tall to my paintball party.

"Cool! I always wondered what they used this old warehouse for!" It's hard to impress Bart so he must like this.

Dad plays so we have three on three.

"Ouch!" The shots sting but this is a blast! Mom and my sisters watch. Braden didn't come because he's with Matt, his personal care attendant. Our family counselor wants Braden to spend time away from us to develop his independence and give us a break. I bet Matt hears a lot about stickers and ends up counting a lot of oddball things. Every other weekend, Braden goes to Grandpa's, and I use that time to have friends over.

After the paintball "war" we go to Tony's Pizza.

"The guys got together and made you a present, Zach," Bart announces.

It's weird knowing that Phinney and Bart are here together and that they actually worked on a gift together. Bart hands me a cardboard box with a green bow taped to it. No wrapping paper. I open it and take out a notebook.

"We know your English journal burned up in your house fire, so we got you a new one, says Justin.

"And what's all this stuff?" I lift a stack of papers out of the box. There are at least a hundred wrinkled sheets and the guys all howl.

Bart says, "Oh, that's the stuff that's worth a million bucks! The entire English class was willing to give up their stash of Monica's poems just so you could start a collection of your own. So there you are!"

Too Tall hands me a big yellow envelope that smells like someone doused it with a gallon of perfume. "You can glue her poems into that notebook and glue this onto the cover." The guys are all snickering.

I slide out a huge colored photo of Monica all nuzzled on my shoulder at the school dance. My face grows warm, and the guys can't stop laughing. The photo is signed with lipstick. *All my love, Monica.*

Eva asks, "Is this Marilyn Monroe's sister?" Her comment brings the house down with laughter.

"I want cake and ice cream," Eva yells from the backseat on the way home. Carly chimes in, and pretty soon all of us are chanting, "I scream, you scream, we all scream for ice cream!"

Grandpa meets us at the house. It is sad to see him come alone. Just before I'm ready to blow out the candles on the leaning-tower-of-cake Mom baked, the doorbell rings.

"SURPRISE!"

It's Grace! Her father and Mr. Salzmann came, too. I take a few seconds to look at them. I can't believe I thought they were bad people.

After making a wish, I blow out my 13 candles. As Mom is passing out the cake and ice cream, Braden and Matt come in the kitchen door.

"H-h-h-appy birthday, Zachary."

The pint-sized kitchen is packed with a dozen people, but no one minds.

Mom and Dad give me a new "used" bike. "You should be happy I was along, Zach. Your Dad wanted to buy you one that looked like his when he was your age; it weighed about 50 pounds and had only one speed," giggles Mom.

"Yes. Slow!" adds Dad, which gets a laugh from everyone.

Mr. Salzmann gives me a new pair of binoculars. "A true neighborhood watchman needs some binoculars." I struggle to hold back the emotion I feel about this, considering how wrong I have been about the guy. Last week our family was invited to his backyard for the dedication of the wooden statue he carved of his daughter. It's exactly the size she was when she was killed. The details of her face and hands are amazing. The way the Salzmann family has turned a horrible tragedy into something wonderful gives me hope for myself.

Carly and Eva hand me a jar of jellybeans, and Grandpa gives me a picture of Hank and Beulah. I quickly put the picture of the dogs down before I can think about them. I turn and open Braden's present. It's an envelope with stickers all over it. He actually gave them up for my birthday card. I take out the handwritten note and read it aloud.

The fire chief is giving me an award for helping use my key to open the door during the fire. I want you to bring me to the awards ceremony. Happy Birthday to the best brother ever.

My voice breaks on the last words, and I have to take a few seconds before I can speak again. "Awesome, bro!" I look at him but he is looking at the floor. "I'd love to go!" I would hug Braden but he wouldn't like it.

"Our present is an announcement!" Grace says excitedly.

"I have been offered a job in Chicago," Grace's dad says proudly.

Oh no. She's moving.

"But there has been enough change in our lives the past year. So, we have decided to stay in Hazard."

I squeeze my eyes shut in relief.

"I have had another offer to join the law firm of Adams and Meyer right here in town. I just leased a townhouse about a mile from here."

Wow. That candle wish thing works fast!

"And the best part is that Avery gets to come and live with us again!" Grace hops up and down and squeals.

"So you'll be around to go to the movie on Saturday?" I give her a look that shows her I haven't forgotten.

"Only if there's popcorn with extra butter."

I want to wrap my arms around her. But I just sigh a huge sigh and smile. Her eyes are sparkling back at me and it is enough. For now.

I used to think Braden and his treasures were useless.
—Zach

Braden's bedroom is on the main floor with Mom and Dad. I hear music coming from his room, so I wander in. He is sitting cross-legged on the floor with his newest superhero shirt and sunglasses on. The fire chief's medal hangs from his neck. An old phone book is on his lap. His sticker collection was lost in the fire, so he's started a new one. He has about forty erasers lined up along the rug. Erasers shaped like pigs and cars, soccer balls, and rainbows. A new collection.

The eight keys I found are neatly laid out on his windowsill.

Without looking up at me he says, "What?"

"Oh nothing. Just thought I'd come and say hi."

"Well then say it."

"Hi, Braden." And I can't help but smile.

He starts numbering his notebook pages. Mom bought him two new ones.

"Help me." It's more of an expectation than a demand.

"What should I do?"

"Hold the pages open." I can do that.

The song "Can't Stop the Feeling" is playing. "What happened to "Believer", Braden?"

"It burned up." No emotion, just the facts.

I bite my lip. How can it bother me so much and not faze him?

My eyes settle on the framed picture on the dresser of Braden shaking the fire chief's hand. I don't remember being more proud than I was that day. I used to think Braden and his treasures were useless.

After about thirty pages, I kneel beside him. "You know, Braden, if they lined up all the ninth-graders in Hazard and I got to choose one to be my LINK, you know who I'd pick?"

A long pause. I don't know if he's registered my question. Finally he stops writing and stares at my chest as if deep in thought.

"Annabelle."

This cracks me up. When I'm done laughing, I say,

"NO! *You.* I'd pick you. I'd pick my SuperBro."

Without looking at me, he flatly says, "I'd pick you, too," and goes back to numbering.

Epilogue

I haven't been in Mr. Dunphey's room for two years. It looks the same and he does too. There are no piñatas dangling from the ceiling today. I look at the light that Braden killed. It's been repaired of course, and no one would know from looking at it that it had been attacked.

It's LINK Day, and my ninth-grade homeroom class with Miss Thompson has been paired with Mr. Dunphey's seventh-graders. Grace smiles at me from where she is standing by her LINK, Ella. We are halfway through the pairings, and it is my turn.

"My name is Zach and my LINK is Cedric Allen." I smile and walk over to Cedric and kneel beside his wheelchair. Cedric makes a sharp, cawing sound and his eyes are dancing with joy. I reach out to high five him, and his twisted hand makes an attempt to meet mine.

A few weeks ago when we were filling out our LINK profiles, I wrote a note on mine asking if there were any seventh graders who had special challenges. Miss Thompson told me about Cedric.

Cedric was born with cerebral palsy. He has trouble controlling his muscles and movements. His speech is difficult to understand, so he uses an electronic communication board to have a conversation.

"Can I be his LINK?"

I didn't think Miss Thompson was ever going to answer me. "Are you sure?"

Smiling, I told her, "Yes, it's fine."

And for the first time in my life, I believe it.

Selected Bibliography

Listed here are the standout selections of writings and music that I have referred to and borrowed from in the construction of my novel, *Finding SAM*.

Books

Erickson, John R. *The Original Adventures Of Hank The Cowdog.* Perryton, TX: Maverick Books, 1983.

Hinton, S. E. *The Outsiders.* New York City: Viking Press, 1967.

Lee, Harper. *To Kill A Mockingbird.* Philadelphia: Lippincott, 1960.

Glenday, Craig. *Guinness Book Of Records.* Vancouver: Jim Pattison Book Group, 2015.

Poems

Frost, Robert. "Nothing Gold Can Stay." As reprinted by Hinton, S. E. *The Outsiders.* New York City: Viking Press, 1967. Chapter 5.

Songs

Beatles, The. "Hey Jude." By John Lennon and Paul McCartney. Single A-side; B-side *Revolution.* London: Apple Records, 1968. Vinyl.

Diamond, Neil. "Sweet Caroline." By Neil Diamond. *Brother Love's Travelling Salvation Show.* Hollywood: Uni Records, 1969. Vinyl.

Imagine Dragons. "Believer." By Dan Reynolds, Wayne Sermon, Ben McKee, Daniel Platzman, Justin Tranter and its producers Mattman & Robin. *Evolve.* Nashville: Interscope Records and Kindinacorner, 2017. Vinyl.

Journey. "Don't Stop Believin'." By Jonathan Cain, Steve Perry, Neal Schon. *Escape*. New York City: Columbia Records, 1981. Vinyl.

Los del Rio. "Macarena." By Rafael Ruiz Perdigones, Antonio Romero Monge, SWK. *A Mí Me Gusta*. New York City: RCA Records, 1995. Vinyl.

Perri, Christina. "A Thousand Years." By Christina Perri and David Hodges. *The Twilight Saga: Breaking Dawn—Part 1: Original Motion Picture Soundtrack*. New York City: Atlantic Records, 2011. Digital Download.

Perry, Katy. "Firework." By Katy Perry, Stargate, Sandy Wilhelm and Ester Dean. *Teenage Dream*. Atlanta: Soapbox Studios, 2010. Digital Download.

Village People, "Y.M.C.A." By Jacques Morali, Victor Willis. *Cruisin'*. New York City: Casablanca Records, 1978. Vinyl.

Television

BBC Worldwide, prod. *Dancing With The Stars*. ABC, CBS Television City, Los Angeles. 1 June 2005–present.

Disney Television Animation, prod. *Phineas and Ferb*. Disney-ABC, Los Angeles. 2007-2015.

Film

Happy Feet. Dir. George Miller. Perf. Elijah Wood, Robin Williams. Warner Bros. Pictures, 2006. Film.

Author's Note

Finding S.A.M. isn't a book about autism. It is a story about how it might be for an almost 13-year-old to be longing for a carefree life and realizing it doesn't work that way. But here's the backstory.

I started writing this story after our youngest child graduated from high school. My husband and I had "made it" through the tough years of realizing something wasn't quite right when he still wasn't speaking as a toddler, when his (lack of) social skills caused tangles with siblings and neighbors, and when he finally got the diagnosis of autism. We were vigilant about getting him all the support he needed, but didn't want his needs and services to be at the expense of our other kids' well being. I wish I could say the plan worked, but once again, "it doesn't work that way." No matter what, we couldn't insulate them from the fact that their brother was different and would forever be that way. As a mother, I worried about how autism would affect all our children.

There is no question that disabilities affect families, friendships, and futures. What I didn't realize when our son was young, is how that impact would become a positive one. Inspiration and admiration are two words that float to the surface. The lives of those who know our son have been enriched and changed in a way I never imagined. This book isn't our family story, but I stirred up a slice of both the angst and the joy we experienced and created a new one in *Finding S.A.M.* Although I wrote it for middle-grade readers, who are often in the thick of the awkward years, the message will resonate with all who have endured a struggle with a situation they have little control over. Some of this book is uncomfortable. Some of it is funny. All of it is life.

I write to give readers a chance to recognize that their emotions are empowering and can lead to change. This story is about longing and loss, but also about so much more. It is about acceptance, hope, and most importantly, dignity. It highlights the notion that every one matters. Readers of *Finding S.A.M.* will recognize that circumstances and people are not always as they appear; they will be happily shocked to see misperceptions blown away and to learn that an individual least expected to contribute can indeed make extraordinary contributions.

A book is a group effort. I want to express gratitude to Keith Garton, Jennifer Walters, the design team, and all the talented crew at Red Chair Press for bringing this story to you. Their expertise and dedication to making books that make a difference for young readers is inspiring.

So, What Is Autism Anyway?

by Elizabeth Verdick

My child was diagnosed with autism at age two. I had so many questions. *How did this happen? Why did it happen?* But most of all, *what do we do now?* He was young, and Early Intervention—expert help in communication, social skills, and behavior—was the key to my son's learning. Watching him work so hard every day, all I could think was, "He's my hero." I wanted to write a book for my son and children like him, and I worked with a doctor to make that happen. Elizabeth Reeve, MD, and I wrote *The Survival Guide for Kids with Autism Spectrum Disorders* so we could reach out to children and families like ours. Dr. Reeve has worked with young people with autism for 30 years, and she too has raised a son who has autism.

Today, experts use the term Autism Spectrum Disorder (ASD) or autism to describe a group of symptoms that add up to the diagnosis. As you can see, the word *spectrum* appears in the term (*spectrum* means a *wide range*). Doctors check to see if the person experiences challenges in three main areas (1) communication, (2) social skills, and (3) repetitive or restricted behaviors. How each individual shows symptoms can be highly individualistic.

For example, one child might be very verbal, while another is mostly nonverbal. One might seem shy in social situations, while another might stand quite close or speak in a loud voice. One child might tend to deeply focus on a favorite topic, hobby, or collection, which feels exciting or relaxing. Another might flap, spin, or engage in a repetitive behavior as a way to feel calm. It varies so much! This quote helps put things in perspective: "If you've met one person with autism, you've met *one* person with autism."

A few things to know:

- Every person with autism is unique.
- The challenges for a person who's "on the spectrum" may be mild or serious.
- Those with autism have a broad range of differences that may change over time.
- People with ASD will always have ASD.

Not long ago, another term was commonly in use to describe autism: Asperger's syndrome. Sometimes, people would simply call it "Asperger's." The terminology is still out there, but doctors no longer use it. So, you may know a person who has Asperger's, which means the individual has autism. This can all be confusing! The important thing to know is that a person who has ASD, or any mental-health condition, is still an individual—not a collection of symptoms. Not a label. Not someone who should only be defined by this one aspect of who he or she is.

Experts know that autism tends to affect boys more than girls. As of today, the Centers for Disease Control (CDC) say autism affects an estimated 1 in 59 children in the United States. However, this number changes from time to time due to rising diagnoses. Doctors are still trying to learn what causes autism. To keep things simple: it is known that parents pass on genes that can make a child more susceptible to having autism. There are also environmental triggers of some kind, still not fully understood.

Having a child with autism creates challenges for the whole family. Parents are often confused and overwhelmed by both the diagnosis and the interventions. Parents might think they aren't doing enough—and may not know where to turn. Emotions run high in all families at times, but especially in those affected by ASD. The person with autism may have difficulties with learning, or with handling anger, frustration, and other negative feelings. Siblings see and feel that happening. They bear witness to the struggles while facing the challenges of growing up in a family that's "different." This may make life more difficult for a sibling—but you know what else? Many of these siblings grow up with a greater sense of caring and understanding, and become more responsible. They often act as their brother's or sister's biggest supporter, knowing just how far that person has come.

All of us, who love someone on the spectrum, or work as advocates and helpers, hope that autism awareness will continue to grow. You've become more aware by reading *Finding S.A.M.* If you want more information about autism, please visit the Autism Society at https://www.autism-society.org.

Elizabeth Verdick is a children's book writer and editor. She has authored and coauthored many books including, *Dude, That's Rude!* and *How to Take the Grrrr Out of Anger.* She is also the author of *The Survival Guide for Kids with Autism Spectrum Disorders.* Elizabeth lives near St. Paul, Minnesota, with her husband and their two children.